MANIACS WITH KNIVES

BY SHAUN HUPP

Maniacs with Knives
Copyright: Shaun Hupp
Published: April 2017

Praise for Maniacs with Knives

"A much needed voice in extreme horror."

-Tim Miller, author of Fifty Shades of Hell

"Not your typical horror story. This will make you clench the seat and reach for the lights. Bloody, gruesome and depraved. Totally worth it!"

-Roadie Notes

"An absolute mind fuck of human nature horror from beginning to end! This one is going to be hard to beat in 2017"

-American Mary, Fans of Modern Horror

"Shaun Hupp is a twisty fucker who can really get into the dark places that make my 'creepy girl' parts tingle. Fantastic."

-Rayne Havok, author of XXX

"Probably the most extreme thing I've read in a long time"

-13, Fans of Modern Horror

"Gird your butts."

-Betty Rocksteady, author of Like Jagged Teeth

For David Tamarin,

Never let your dream die. Let it brutally kill you over and over for an audience. Just make sure to get every wound, every scar, and every unnecessary amputation all down between the covers of a book. I'd read the shit out of that. Much love and respect.

And for Becky,

Some people enter our lives and never leave a lasting impact on us. You are not one of those people. You have left a crater in my heart and filled it with love, respect, humor, and above all else, friendship. It's a shame I have to share you with the rest of the world, but it would be unfair to deprive them of you. Keeping on doing what you're doing.

A NOTE TO THE READER

Fuck you. Still with me? Good. Fuck you again.

Let me explain a little about my work. I'm calling it unapologetic horror because I'm tired of apologizing to those who can't handle my writing. This world is becoming full of trigger warnings, and this is yours. Within these pages, you will not find a safe place. This is extreme horror with the emphasis on extreme. You've been warned.

Fuck you.

I'm not here to be your friend. I'm here to mess with your head. As an author, I thought about saying that I was going to 'rape your mind,' but that wouldn't be true. You bought, borrowed, or stole this book. You opened its pages. You are a consenting adult. There is no rape involved. I'll tell you right now that this book contains depravity, bloodshed, and psychological torture for not only the characters but the reader as well.

I tried to stop you.

You're going to turn the page.

I'm not sorry.

Shaun Hupp

CONTENTS

MANIACS WITH KNIVES

BY SHAUN HUPP

Chapter One

Meet the Maniacs

"Hello? Is anyone there?"

Erin couldn't see anything. At first, she thought she was blindfolded or that something was covering her face. That wasn't true. She had shaken her head when she had first woken up and felt nothing covering it. Her eyes weren't blocked or shut. They were open. Darkness was all she could see.

Where am I?

More concerning was the question of why were her hands tied behind her back. She tried to move her feet but found they were also bound. Once she got her equilibrium focused, Erin realized that she was facing upward. She was lying on a bed. The mattress beneath her stank of urine and something else, something familiar. Erin gagged as she breathed it in and realized that she couldn't feel any clothes on her body. The bed felt moist against her bare skin.

"Is this some kind of joke? Real funny, Ja-"

Jake. Now, I remember.

She was out on a date with her boyfriend, Jake. They had went out to the movies since it was a Friday. Her parents wouldn't let her go out on school nights, but that was coming to an end. Graduation was just around the corner, and soon she would be off to college. She and Jake had talked about getting an apartment off campus. Luckily, they were going to the same school. Everything seemed to be going perfectly.

And now this.

"Hello? Anyone?"

Erin closed her eyes, remembering that you can adjust your eyes to the dark if you keep them closed for thirty seconds. She began to count, slowing down slightly as the numbers climbed. She wasn't so sure she wanted to see her surroundings. It was at eighteen the black on the inside of her eyelids turned red. She opened her eyes and was staring at a single lightbulb swinging above her head from a chain.

"Hello? Who's there? This isn't funn-"

Looking around, she saw the mattress. The smell she couldn't identify earlier, the coppery smell that she thought she recognized, was partially-dried blood and the mattress was covered in it. A scream came from the back of her throat but was quickly snuffed out by a hand that was slapped across her lips.

"Hush now. We can't have you ruining those vocal chords of yours."

The man appeared at her side. He looked in his late forties with graying hair and beard. He was tall and thin to the point he looked emaciated. His dirty clothes hung from his frame as if he was a wire hanger.

"There will be plenty of time for screaming later." He removed his hand but kept it close just in case she screamed again. When he was satisfied, he sat down in the chair next to the bed. "I suppose you're a little confused about how you ended up here."

Where was here?

She looked past him and saw pale gray bricks. The ceiling where the bulb hung was plain drywall. In front of her, there was a table and chair set. There were no windows. Only a single door offered her any sort of hope.

I'm in his basement.

"Are. . . Are you going to kill me?"

The man laughed. It was a great booming laugh despite his size and age. After several seconds, a fit of coughing took over. "Now, there's the million dollar question: Am I going to kill you? No. I'm not going to kill you. Well, I shouldn't say that. You know how people never say, 'I'm dying' but really they are. We all are eventually. It just won't happen for a really long time. Think about this situation in the same way. I'm going to kill you. . . Just not for a really long time."

Erin started sobbing. "Why!? What did I do?"

"I see something in you. You're stunning. I don't see any tattoos or piercings on you. You're flawless. Even your long, red hair looks like your natural color from what I've seen on the rest of your body. You don't see that too often anymore. Everyone wants to put a hole in their body or cover their skin with gaudy art." He stood up and walked toward the foot of the bed where the table was. Erin's eyes never left him. He kept his back to her. "You, my dear, are a blank canvas. The art I put on your body will not be gaudy. I will make you even more beautiful."

He turned around. In his hands, he held a silver tray that contained several large knives. Each was spotless and looked brand new. Erin feared that wasn't the case.

"Though I'm afraid I might have to add a few holes."

The holes of the showerhead came to life, shooting out water as the knob was turned full blast. Jen leaned her head back and pulled her long, black hair behind her, letting the hot stream spray against her chest. Her hands, now covered in her favorite lavender soap, began lathering her breasts. The suds slowly slid down her flat stomach, lingered at her pubic mound, traveled the length of her long legs, and gathered at the drain. She let out a moan as she squeezed her breast together. She closed her eyes. In her mind, her hands were Troy's. One of her hands followed the same path as the suds, stopping when she reached her vagina. She gently inserted a finger inside, finding herself already wet. It had nothing to do with the shower.

"Oh, Troy," she whispered, then realized that with her parents not home, there was no need to be quiet. She pushed another finger in. "Troy!"

As her fingers slipped in and out, she pictured in her mind all the things she wanted Troy to do to her when he came over later. In a discrete, black bag under her bed, she had her outfit ready for tonight. Jen felt weird going into that store a week ago. She didn't know what to expect because all its windows were covered in cheap blinds. Luckily, the cashier working that day was female, and there was no one else in the store. Her biggest fear was being ogled by a bunch of perverts. Knowing time probably wasn't on her side, she quickly made her way to the intimate apparel section. She found her size in a lacy, red outfit that she wasn't even sure what to call. The cashier must have noticed how embarrassed she was and barely spoke to her when she rang her up. Jen was grateful.

She and Troy had been a couple for several months now. They had both been each other's firsts, but Jen suspected if the rumors were true, she wasn't really his first. It didn't matter, though. She was in love. They hadn't official said it yet, but she had a feeling after tonight, he might just utter those three little words. She would make sure he forgot the names of any other girls he had been with.

Her fingers moved faster. She felt her body begin to tremble as her moans intensified. Her hand left her breast and reached out to grab ahold of the shower rack to steady herself. She imagined Troy thrusting into her. His strong arms holding her down. His body pressed against hers. She screamed out as her orgasm shot through her body.

She smiled, feeling her body return to normal. She was still horny and didn't mind one bit.

I can't wait for him to show up.

But there were three things Jen was unaware of.

First of all, she didn't realize the handwriting on the note left by her parents was not her parents'. They were not going to spend the night out at a fancy restaurant. Inside, they would be spending the evening stuffed in the trash can in the garage, their limbs separated from their bodies and stuffed into garbage bags.

Secondly, she didn't realize that Troy wasn't coming over. While she was showering, a text was sent from her phone saying she had to cancel, that her parents were staying home now. He was crushed, and so was the phone, now in two pieces on the floor.

And last of all, she didn't see the man that was watching her the entire time she was in the shower. Nor did she see the meat cleaver in his hand, still covered in fresh blood.

"Stop me if you've heard this one. A guy walks into a bar. . ."

"Please. Are you serious? Is this what our conversation has resorted to? Bad jokes?"

Alex didn't know what to say. The two men had sat at the bar all afternoon, and Alex was the one doing most of the talking. He was a regular at this bar, but he had never seen this guy before. "So, what do you want to talk about, big guy?"

The other man was named Owen. Other than that, Alex didn't know much about him except that he didn't live around here and he liked whiskey. It didn't even seem to faze him no matter how much he drank. It was probably due to his size. He easily dwarfed anyone else in the room, and it was all muscle.

"We've been here for hours, grandpa. Don't you have some tales of the olden days to regale me with."

Alex laughed. While he probably had a good twenty years on his twenty-something drinking partner, he never considered himself a 'grandpa.' He guessed if anyone in the room compared them, they might see it. Alex certainly let himself go over the years. His full head of hair had started to retreat with all the stress his life had brought him. He knew the guy on the barstool next to him would one day be where he was at. "I've got plenty of stories. You just wouldn't believe them."

"Try me."

Alex started to say something and then changed his mind. "Nevermind. Hey. How about that terrorist attack in Spain yesterday? That was something. I never thought-"

"I don't care about all that. Quit stalling. Tell me. You got some secrets, old man?"

The guy was starting to piss him off. Taking another drink, Alex shook his head. "Like I said, you wouldn't believe it. It's getting late. We've both had a lot to drink. Maybe we should just call it a night."

Owen stared at the man, then threw back another shot of whiskey. "Pussy." He put down a wad of cash for the bartender and stood up to leave.

"Wait! Wait. . ."

Owen sat back down and stared at him. His mannerisms suggested that he was waiting to be impressed.

"If there's one thing I'm not, it's a pussy. I've never told anyone this before. You've got to swear to me not to tell anyone else."

The big man nodded. "I swear."

"I'm the Bay River Slasher."

"I'm sorry, honey. I didn't mean to-"

"What!? You didn't mean to do what? Ruin dinner? Because that's what you did," Kimberly's husband yelled as he threw the plate of food at the wall. It shattered, sending food and broken pieces of porcelain all over the floor. "Now. Clean this mess up."

Rich stormed off, leaving Kim sobbing over the sink. The argument had started when she placed dinner down in front of him. She knew he would be mad. She knew the meat was burnt. She had gotten careless and made a mistake. She had gotten busy with other chores and forgot to check on the meatloaf.

The past couple of months hadn't been easy for either of them. Rich had lost his job awhile back, so Kim had to pick up shifts whenever she could at the diner. Her husband took some temp jobs when they came his way, but so far, he had yet to land anything permanent. He spent most of his days job hunting.

Richard had a temper, and his favorite way to take out his aggression was to leave bruises on her body. She could handle it, though. She loved him, and she knew deep down that he loved her. He always apologized after he hit her and she'd forgive him. It was part of their ritual. That was then. Now, it seemed like the stress of being out of work had escalated his anger. Particularly, the past couple of days had been rough. Kim assumed he must have thought he had a job lined up and it fell through.

It's not like he talks to me anymore.

Kim stared out the window. She wondered if maybe this relationship was a mistake. They had only been married for five years. She shuddered to think what it would be like in another five. It was not getting any better. They both met much later in life. He was a failed musician turned workaholic who decided he wanted to settle down. She was previously married, only to be divorced when she and her then-husband found out she couldn't have children.

She was devastated but thought they could move on. Her husband did. With a new woman.

Maybe I can move on again.

She wasn't sure if that was possible. She knew every year that went by just made it harder to find someone to be with. Kim was so excited when the online dating site matched her up with Rich. After numerous failed attempts, she convinced herself that she would get her 'happily ever after' and she would do whatever it took.

Like being turned into a punching bag.

"Honey?"

Kim turned around, ready to accept her husband's apology as she had done a million times before. They would hug. He'd kiss her on the cheek. He'd wipe her tears away. He'd promise never to do it again.

"Why haven't you fucking cleaned up the floor like I told you!?"

"I. . . I," Kim was shocked. This wasn't normal. She knew he had been acting differently this week, but she hadn't expected this.

"I. I. I. Stop studdering, bitch! Fucking clean this shit up!"

He clenched his fists and rushed toward her. Without thinking, her right hand reached back and grabbed a butcher knife from the knife block. Before she knew what she was doing, she had the blade handle-deep in Richard's stomach. All the rage drained from his face, along with its color. He stumbled backward, clutching his stomach. Blood poured from the wound as he tried to make it to the telephone on the wall. Whether it was the blood, or the food, or the shards of plate, Rich's foot slipped out from beneath him before he could make it. His head smacked hard against the tile. His bloody hand struck the wallpaper, trying to reach for the phone. Kim watched as each strike, each handprint got weaker and weaker until his arm finally hit the floor.

She stood there in silence, listening for him to say something, listening for the sound of his breathing. There was nothing. The room was silent. Then, Kim started laughing. First, it was a little chuckle and then, it became uncontrollable. She looked down at the meatloaf that was now soaked red with blood. It had dawned on her.

"Ketchup. This probably could have been avoided if we had ketchup."

Chapter Two

Mocking the Maniacs

The man chuckled.

"I'm serious," Erin said, trying to wiggle her hands free from the cord that bound them. "People will be looking for me. My parents, my boyfriend. They will all be looking for me."

"Let them look."

Erin was quiet. The man seemed serious with his statement. *Is he right? Is this basement so hidden no one would think to look here? He didn't seem to worry about me yelling for help.*

Thinking she had to try a new tactic, she said,"W. . . What's your name?"

The gaunt man grinned, his flesh bunching up at his cheek bones. His teeth were an aged chessboard: Yellowed molars intermixed with gaps. He was not only Erin's nightmare but a dentist's too. "That, my dear, is not something you need to know."

"But what do I call you?" Erin thought maybe she could reason with the man if she could somehow connect with him. He probably didn't get out much. He was probably lonely.

"You can call me Ben for all I care. Though I'm hoping the world will recognize me by something great. Maybe 'the Artist.' That has a ring to it."

"So, you want fame?"

"Yes. I want to be known throughout the world for my work. I'm hoping that you, my blank canvas, will be my greatest masterpiece." Ben stared down at the tray of knives in front of him as if he were trying to decide on a dish at his favorite restaurant.

Think, Erin. Think.

"And what happens if I can't be the canvas you want me to be? What happens if I'm not a masterpiece when you're finished?"

He looked up from the tray and frowned, looking defeated.

It's working.

"What if I can't bring you the fame you want?"

Ben's frown disappeared, and he shrugged. "No harm. No foul. I'll just find another canvas."

Erin stared blankly at him. "But I. . . I. . ."

"Oh, I'm sorry. I didn't mean to make you think you were special earlier. While I have high hopes for you, I'm afraid you are hardly the first woman I've had in here. You should have realized that by the state of that mattress."

Erin was quiet. *Shit.*

"If you want, later I can show you the other room where I keep my 'failed projects.' We can count them. I bet there's at least a dozen. I'll warn you, though: the smell isn't the greatest."

"No," Erin said, trying to remain calm, trying to remain friendly to the madman, but inside her head, she was screaming in terror. "I believe you. I don't need to see them."

Ben smiled again. "Good. And guess what? I think I've finally decided how to get started." He picked up a strange looking object. It looked like a pair of pliers, but with an extra handle.

"Do you know what this is?"

Erin shook her head.

"It's a Costotome. It's used for cutting ribs. Surgeons would grip onto these two handles to have the equipment grab onto a rib. Then once that was locked into place, they would use this third lever to operate the blade."

"Please. . . No."

"Oh, don't worry. I'm not planning on touching your ribs with this. Oh, heaven's no. That's not what I generally use this for. Maybe one day I'll use it on a rib cage, but for right now, it works pretty damn good on fingers."

Jen's fingers gripped the shower knob and turned it off. She knew she had spent way too much time in there as it was. If her parents were home, they would have yelled at her for wasting water.

And if they found out what I had in mind for later, they'd be even madder.

She opened the glass door and grabbed the towel that was hanging on the hook nearby. After drying herself off, she hopped onto the bathroom rug and peered around the corner. The digital clock on her dresser said, '8:09.'

"Shit!"

Jen hadn't realized she spent so much time in the shower touching herself. She had told Troy to be at her house around 8:30, but she knew he liked to come early.

Hopefully not tonight.

She chuckled to herself as she raced to her bed and reached under the frame for the black bag. After a few grabs at nothing but air, she pulled it out and dumped the contents onto her mattress. Jen grabbed the red, lacy thong, put one foot through each of the leg holes, and slid it up to her hips. Next, she grabbed the top and threw it over her head. It looked like a see-through tank top. She repositioned it, so it showed a lot of cleavage but decided to check the mirror to see how it looked.

Going back into the bathroom, she saw the mirror wouldn't do much good in the state it was in. She picked her towel up off the floor and wiped the mirror down as steam had totally fogged it over. Finally satisfied she cleared enough away, she tossed the towel aside and checked herself out, making sure to turn and look over her shoulder.

Damn, girl. Troy is one lucky guy. If he plays his cards right, maybe we-

In the mirror, she saw a dark figure walk by the doorway of her room. Jen jumped and spun around. Her heart was pounding as she looked around for a weapon. Suddenly, a smile crept across her face.

Troy, you sly devil.

Jen had almost forgotten she had confessed this fetish to her boyfriend. She had long fantasized about someone breaking into her house and having their way with her. She had only told one other person about that, and she thought Jen was nuts. Troy said that maybe they could try it sometime. She also remembered that he promised her something special tonight.

Jen grinned ear-to-ear and in a hokey voice said, "Oh, I'm so scared being in this house all by myself. I hope nothing bad happens." She waited, but Troy didn't appear.

Playing hard to get? Well, I guess I'll just have to find you.

She left the bathroom and her room behind and went into the hallway. She looked toward her parent's room but remembered Troy said it would be weird to have sex in their bed. Turning the other way, she saw the other spare bedrooms and the stairs.

Where would you go?

Jen headed toward the stairs. "I think I'll get a glass of water. It's so hot even though I'm wearing so little cl-"

She stopped in her tracks. In front of her on the carpet, lie her cell phone. It was broken in two pieces. It wasn't making any sense to Jen. She couldn't understand why Troy would break her phone.

Then, she saw why.

The man that walked up the stairs was not her boyfriend. Her boyfriend wasn't over six feet. Her boyfriend wouldn't be covered in blood. Her boyfriend wouldn't be wearing the flesh of her father's face as a mask.

"Never heard of him."

"You've never heard of the Bay River Slasher? You've got to be kidding me."

"Nope. Sorry," Owen said as he threw his long hair back, taking another shot of whiskey.

"How could you not have heard of him!? Those killings were nationwide news in the 90s."

He laughed. "The 90s? I was born in the 90s. If you were some big shot, I wouldn't have heard of you. I was probably still sucking on my momma's tit."

Alex couldn't believe it. He always thought of himself as a living legend. He was infamous. He was the most prolific serial killer to never get caught. And now, this stranger was telling him that he was a nobody, that who he was had vanished from everyone's memory.

Alex took a drink and sat at his barstool, defeated. He looked around at all the people in the room laughing and having a good time. During his killing spree, people had locked themselves in their houses. Bars like this one would close up early due to lack of patrons. The streets weren't safe. The police were always on patrol. The Bay River Slasher was feared by the whole country.

Now, nothing.

"So, Mr. Big Shot, you going to talk or what?"

"Excuse me?"

"I wanted to hear a story," Owen said, ordering yet another shot. "Enlighten me on who you used to be."

"Alright," Alex said, thinking about where to start. It had been so long ago, and he had never told anyone his secret before. He looked around at the rest of the bar, thinking that someone else might be listening in on their conversation. No one was paying attention to him.

I've been forgotten.

"It all started on September 25th, 1991. . ."

"Well, Kim. You've certainly fucked things up."

And now, you're talking to yourself. That's surely a sign of psychosis.

"Shut up."

Kim looked down at the body of her husband. In mere minutes, her life as she knew it disappeared. There was no going back after this. No reset button would clean up this mess and raise the dead. She knew she was screwed unless she could prove it was self-defense.

With your history? Doubtful.

"I said shut up!"

She had to figure out how to fix this. Fortunately, she realized that she had quite a bit of time. Rich was unemployed and didn't keep in much contact with friends and family, if at all. Being completely honest with herself, Kim could probably pick up a few more hours now that she didn't have to keep Rich happy and she'd be able to pay most of the bills.

But what about the body? You can't just leave him here like this. Someone could look in that window at any-

"Yes. Yes. I know. I need to clean this up. Then, when I'm thinking more clearly, I can decide how to move forward."

A broom and mop will take care of the floor, but won't do shit for a dead body.

"Well, what do you fucking suggest, voice in my head?"

I suggest you grab a bunch of garbage bags and look for the hacksaw in the garage.

Chapter Three

Knowing your Knives

Erin watched in horror as the costotome clamped down hard onto her pinkie finger. She wished she had put up a fight when he untied her hands from behind her back just to retie them to the posts of the bed. He had held a knife to her throat as he did it and she had no doubt he would use it. Thinking back, maybe it would have been a better way to go.

"Now, you might feel a little pinch." He locked the handles and opened his hand to get a grip on the third handle.

"JAKE!" she yelled out of nowhere. "I was with my boyfriend Jake when you took me. What happened to him?"

Ben laughed. "I wondered when you were going to ask about him. My special blend of knockout juice tends to leave its victims a little fuzzy on the details. You've just got to think real hard, and it'll come back to you."

Keep him talking. Maybe he'll see you as more than a canvas.

Erin shook her head. "I can't. I can't remember anything other than going to the movies with him. I'm worried about him."

"Think back. You two didn't finish your movie. You must have left the showing early, and no other movie was starting soon because you two just happened to find yourself outside the theater when no one else was around. You probably wanted to find someplace a little more secluded. Probably wanted to do what teenagers do late at night. I'm sure he talked you into it. You two were walking in the parking lot-"

"You. . . You asked us for some change."

Ben clapped his hands and jumped up excitedly. Erin was happy that his hand left the costotome. Though, it was still clamped on her finger. "Now, you're starting to remember. Guilty as charged. I pretended to be nothing more than a simple panhandler."

"You asked for change and then. . ,"

A flood of images passed through Erin's head. She saw Jake reaching both hands into his pockets to retrieve some coins. She saw the hobo pull out a pocket knife and slash her boyfriend's throat while he was defenseless. He fell to the asphalt with only gurgling noises coming from his mouth. Erin opened her mouth to scream, but a wet rag quickly covered it. She felt herself get lightheaded and she hit the ground next to Jake. His eyes were wide and vacant. The blood from the wound on his neck crept toward her. She wanted to get away, but couldn't move. Then, there was nothing.

"You killed him. YOU KILLED JAKE!"

Ben frowned. "I know you're upset. It'll pass. I know you probably won't see it yet, but he didn't appreciate you the way I will. I was a young man once. I know what it's like to be a teenage boy. He was only thinking about getting his dick wet. He wanted to use your body for his sick desires. I, on the other hand, want to bring out your true beauty. I want to glorify your body."

His hand gripped the tool once again.

"No! Please."

"I have a good feeling about this. It was fate that brought us together. You're going to be my masterpiece."

He clamped the third handle down. Erin's screams filled the basement however no one would be able to hear them. At the same time, no one could hear Ben utter one simple word.

"Beautiful."

Jen's screams filled the upstairs hallway as the stranger advanced toward her with a meat cleaver raised above his head. She ran back to her bedroom and locked the door behind her. Within seconds, the door shook on its hinges as if it were hit with a sledgehammer. Jen ran to her window but quickly decided against it. She knew from prior experience that there was no climbing out or climbing up as Troy had tried in the past. She could scream for help, thinking it might scare him away.

Guys that wear other people's faces don't get scared.

A long crack formed on the door as it was struck by another blow. Jen knew she'd have to fight to survive, but didn't know what she could use as a weapon. Another crack split the door, and she saw the meat cleaver for a second. Not knowing what else to do, she ran for her bathroom and locked that door behind her. She threw open all the drawers and searched for anything that could cause some damage. She heard her bedroom door finally give out and footsteps heading toward her.

Shit. Shit! SHIT!

The door rocked on its hinges, and all Jen managed to find was a small pair of scissors she sometimes used to trim split ends. The door started to give away with each blow from the cleaver. Jen stood on her bathmat in her new lingerie with her hand gripped on the scissors as if it were a knife.

Finally, a piece of the door fell away. A bloody hand reached through and grabbed for the doorknob. Jen sprang forward, plunged the scissors into the man's hand, and quickly jumped back. The hand retreated taking her only weapon with it. The man never made a sound. In fact, now the whole house was quiet.

Could he have left?

It didn't make sense. Jen knew she couldn't have hurt him that bad. She slowly stepped off the bathmat and went toward the door. Leaning forward, she peered through the gaping hole in the wood.

Nothing.

Still not entirely convinced, Jen pushed her head through the hole so she could get a better view of her bedroom. The hand grabbed a fistful of black hair and pulled. Jen screamed as her shoulders slammed against the part of the door still standing. Her legs uselessly flailed in the air. She tried to use her hands to push against the doorframe to get away, but he was too strong. She looked up at the man wearing her father's flesh. His lips formed a smile between her father's dead lips. It was the most revolting thing she had ever seen and the second to last thing she ever saw.

The last thing was the meat cleaver coming down.

"... And I just couldn't take it anymore." Alex said, slamming his drink down on the bar.

*****

I had a pretty decent life. I had a great job. I had my fair share of women. Still, something was missing. I had these dark urges most of my life, but I had never acted on them. These urges kept building, kept growing, kept pushing to be released.

I finally gave in that day.

I loaded up my car with a bunch of supplies. I had a tarp, duct tape, rope, garbage bags, lots of knives, and most importantly, a plan. I drove out of state and began the hunt for any young women who were hitchhiking. I figured that if they were out on the road, they were less likely to be noticed as missing or they were already listed as a missing person to begin with. Either way, the risk would be much lesser than grabbing someone that might be expected into work the next day or who always calls their mom every night. These runaways had nobody to miss them. If I was going to give in to my dark urges, I was going to make sure I didn't get caught.

As luck would have it, it didn't take long for me to find my first target. I was half-hoping I wouldn't find anyone, that I'd turn around and forget my plans. Maybe I could have fought those urges, and eventually, they'd go away. The other half of me was excited and screamed at me to apply the brakes when I saw her thumb. My foot agreed.

"Where you headed?"

She leaned down to peer into my car through my rolled down window. I could see her eyes searching for something. I knew she might have been attacked in the past, maybe even raped. She probably knew what to look for. Luckily for me, unlucky for her, my supplies were hidden in the trunk.

"As far as you'll take me."

I nodded and unlocked the passenger side door. She got in, and I finally got a good look at her. She had to be in her early twenties. Her long hair was probably golden blonde several years or showers ago. The road had taken its toll on her, and yet, she still was quite beautiful even as thin as she was.

"That's the weird thing to say," I replied. "You've got to be going somewhere?"

She shook her head. "No. Not really. I just want to see the world and traveling by car sure beats hoofing it."

"Fair enough."

The car went silent. I wasn't really sure what to talk about. I wasn't the type of guy who could just start up conversations with strangers. Besides that, my mind was preoccupied with deciding on how I was going to kill her. Small talk was the last thing on my mind as my urges formed dark thoughts in my head.

I felt the car rumble as my tires started to weave onto the shoulder. My gaze had lingered a little too long on my passenger, taking my eyes off the road. I realized it, and so did she. Her body shifted away from me, and she crossed her arms over her small breasts in an attempt to hide them.

Way to go. Now she's got her guard up.

"I think maybe this is far enough. You can stop here."

I looked at the road in front of me. My eyes then went to my rearview mirror.

Sounds good to me.

My foot agreed again and slammed on the brakes. My seatbelt held tight against my chest, protecting me. My passenger's, however, did not because she hadn't put hers on. Maybe this was one of the tricks she had learned on the road. Maybe you're not supposed to wear a seatbelt in case you need to jump out of a car. It didn't matter anymore. Regardless of the reason, she'd never have to worry about who picked her up. She'd never hitchhike again, or do anything else for that matter. Her face hit the dash hard. Her body bounced back into the seat. Blood poured out from her nostrils, and her eyes looked dazed. Not taking any chances, I grabbed a bunch of that dirty blond hair and smashed her head back into the dashboard again and again.

Satisfied she wouldn't cause me any more issues, I made a right-hand turn onto an old country road. It was the middle of the day. I needed some privacy with her. I found another turn off that looked like as good as any and parked behind some trees.

Lana Lane. I laughed as I put her driver's license back into her purse. I wanted to know the name of my first victim. I wanted to know whose name I should look for in the newspapers when her body was found. I did not expect it to sound like some comic book character.

Beggers can't be choosers.

I got out of the car, retrieved my equipment from the trunk, and then grabbed Lana. It was quite easy to carry her over my shoulder. I was pleased. When preparing, I did not take into account the weight of the victim having any outcome. Clearly, the universe was on my side. Now, I could easily find a secluded area in the woods and give in to my urges.

I had considered my options. I thought that I could just kill someone quickly. It would be the safest way to go. I was worried though that I'd waste an opportunity. What if a quick kill didn't calm the urges? Would I have to go out for a second kill immediately? I decided I needed to play it safe, but at the same time, I needed to kill someone in the most brutal way possible. Hopefully, then I could return to my normal life, and I could wait until the urges grew unbearable again.

I found the perfect spot. I threw her limp body on the ground. Only her chest moved with her labored breathing. I carefully set down my black leather bag and unzipped it. The sun managed to find its way through the treetops, managing to make each blade shimmer. This truly was a magical moment.

I returned to Lana and began stripping her. I almost wished I packed a bar of soap so I could give her a bath before I began. She stank of cigarettes and asphalt like a long haul trucker. Surprisingly she still managed to still keep everything shaved. I felt my erection strain against my jeans. I didn't consider this option either during my planning. My urges were to kill. Doing this would fulfill a different kind of urge, but I could do that on my own.

Could I combine the two?

I started to unzip.

I heard footsteps.

I quickly scooped up my bag and hid behind a tree. I listened as the sound grew closer and made sure I was completely hidden, but could still see whoever approached. A hunter in camouflage appeared at the edge of the clearing. He nearly dropped his rifle when he saw the naked woman on the ground. He rushed to her and checked her pulse. Just like I had, he put her over his shoulder and carried her back the way he came.

Shit.

I needed to act fast. If I let her go, she could describe my car and me to the police. For as suspicious as she was, she might have even memorized my plate number when I pulled my car off to the side of the road in front of her. I had to do something.

"Lana?" My voice surprised myself. "LANA!"

The hunter stopped and turned to me. I ran toward him. "Oh, thank God you found her. I was so worried."

"You know her?"

I nodded. "Yes. We got separated, and I've been looking for her."

He grunted and spit. "Why's she naked?"

Shit.

"We were. . .uhh. . . role playing. She's my girlfriend. She must have gotten lost and got hurt somehow," I lied.

The hunter nodded as if he understood. He lowered her to the ground. "Crazy kids. This is ma hunting property. I could have shot you thinking you's a deer or sumthing."

I knelt down next to Lana and acted as if I cared about her. "I'm so sorry. We didn't realize-"

I felt the barrel of his rifle press against the side of my head. "Like I said, you's both is trespassing. I think you owe me for not shooting you dead."

I slowly stood up, while the man kept his rifle on me. I held my hands up. "Look. We don't want any trouble. We'll just be on our-"

"No. I could've shot you's both or called the sheriff. You owe me. My house is a mile or so that way. I think we can come to an arrangement."

It clicked in my head as I saw the way his eyes lingered on Lana's naked frame. I couldn't believe it. What were the odds that I'd try to do my first kill only to end up dead at the hands of another psycho?

"Look. I'll level with you," I told him. "I don't know her. I brought her out here to murder her."

The hunter looked stunned and then, he laughed. "You? You don't look like no Ted Bundy."

I frowned. I might not have the look, but that's part of my cover. Like Ted Bundy, I could hide in plain sight. "It's true. I have a murder kit with knives and garbage bags behind that tree."

His gazed followed my fingertip. "Show me then, killer."

I led him to the tree and pointed to my bag. Hesitantly, he crouched down, looking inside. He pulled out a leather binder and opened it. Within, he saw my set of knives strapped down. It was supposed to be for a traveling chef, but I was going to use them for a much darker purpose.

"You're missing one," he said, pointing to an empty elastic strap.

"No. I'm not."

I sprang forward, pulling the knife from my belt. The hunter raised his rifle up, but I was already on him. I brought the blade down on his fingers, slicing through to the bone, causing him to drop his gun. With his good hand, he managed to rock me with a straight punch to the jaw. Dazed, he knocked me back and went for his gun again. I kicked it away and drove my knife into his shoulder. He made a grab for the knife, and we both ended up on the ground with him on top. I still had the knife, but he was pushing the blade toward my neck with all of his weight. I managed a dirty shot by kneeing him in the groin. His body crumpled, and I pushed him off me. Seizing the opportunity, I climbed on top of him, pinned his arms down with my legs, and plunged my knife into the soft skin of his neck over and over. When I finally stopped, I had damn-near decapitated him. I looked at all the blood covering my clothes and laughed. I had my first kill, and it wasn't at all who I expected.

"GET UP!"

My head whipped around, and I found myself staring down the barrel of that same rifle, only now it was being held by my naked hitchhiker.

"I said GET UP!"

Once again, I raised my hands and stood up. She looked at the knife in my hand, and I reluctantly dropped it. "Look. I know we got off on the wrong foot, but I saved you."

"You saved me? You saved me!?"

"Yes. The old perv was going to have his way with you. I stopped him."

"And you weren't going to have your way with me. I was starting to come around earlier. I was pretending to be still knocked out. You were the one that took my clothes off."

29

Shit.

"I. . . I. . ."

"Strip."

"Excuse me?"

"You heard me. I said strip. I want to see you humiliated like I am before I put a bullet in your head."

It sounded like she meant it. I started to take my clothes off. My shirt was the hardest as it was drenched in blood. Finally, I stood in front of her naked. I almost laughed at my farmer's tan made from gore rather than sunlight.

"There. Is this what you wanted to see?"

I waited and then, I saw it. Or I saw the very lack of *it.* I saw *it* whenever I looked in the mirror. I saw *it* when I fought with the hunter. She didn't have *it.* She could threaten me all day, but she didn't have the nerve to pull the trigger. The killer instinct was not in her. Some people have it. Some don't. And some, like me, fight to control it.

I crouched down and retrieved my knife. The gun shook in her hands. "HEY! Don't move! Drop that!"

I stood up and smiled. Slowly, I walked toward her and she, in turn, stepped backward. Unfortunately for her, she wasn't watching her step. She tripped over a rock that was behind her. The rifle flew from her hands, and before she could recover, I was on her.

Her kicking, clawing, and screaming did nothing to stop me. My knife entered her. My penis entered her. I decided to combine those two urges, and I'm glad I did. Her blood lubricated my thrusts. While she was taking her final breath, I was shaking from the best orgasm I had ever had. When I finally came out of the murderous frenzy that took over, I looked down at Lana. I laughed when I saw I wasn't even in her vagina or her asshole anymore. I had carved out a new hole in her stomach and had ejaculated within her intestines. The mixture of red and white formed a creampie in her gut.

I stood up and wiped the blood off my knife. I stared at my reflection in the blade, admiring the man I had become. *It* was there. Blood covered my nude body so much so that it reminded me of when a baby was born. I smiled. That was pretty much me as well. Standing naked in the woods, covered in gore, I was reborn.

*****

"And you know the funniest part of all this?"

"What?" Owen asked as he threw back another shot.

"I was wrong. I thought the urges would be fulfilled by those murders. I thought they would diminish. I thought I could go a few years without killing anyone. Nope. It didn't happen that way at all. The urges just got worse. It was like a drug. I couldn't wait for my next hit, my next kill."

"Are you going to do this or what?"

Kim stared down at the hacksaw in her hand, then looked back up at herself in the mirror.

"The longer you wait," her reflection said, "the harder it's going to be. You're still in shock from killing him. It'll numb the act of what comes next. . . You know. . . cutting apart his body."

Kim didn't know if it was a good or bad sign that the voice wasn't so much inside her head now, but coming from the mirror. Either way, she knew something inside of her snapped. It was a weird feeling, knowing you've gone crazy and you're totally aware of it.

"Where should I start? It's not like I've ever done this before?"

"And you think I have?" the reflection joked. "Cut that bastard's head off. Once that's done, the rest should be a piece of cake."

"Okay. . . If you say so."

Kim turned to her bathtub/shower combo. The shower curtain hung in front of Richard's body. After dragging his limp body up the stairs and throwing him in the tub, she closed the curtain and tried to make a run for it. She didn't want to go through with it. Her reflection stopped her.

Finally, pulling back the shower curtain that was covered in happy ducks, she saw her husband's dead body. The porcelain was already stained pink. She reached down and grabbed a small handful of hair and pressed the serrated blade against his throat. She saw her reflection in the silver of the tub's faucet. She nodded at Kim. Kim nodded back.

With no heart to pump, the blood oozed from the gash as she started to saw back and forth, cutting a little bit deeper each time. Flesh split. Tendons snapped. Kim knew she had hit bone, but she had to keep going. She pushed the hacksaw harder against his neck and sped up her back and forth motion.

"You can do this, Kim," the reflection said still appearing in the faucet, watching her every move. "I believe in you. Just a little bit more."

The blade hit porcelain as she finally cut all the way through. The head pulled free from Rich's body, and Kim held his face up to hers. She dropped the hacksaw onto his chest, never breaking her stare at the head of her abusive husband.

"I did it. I did it! You hear that, Rich? You said I couldn't do anything right, but I did this. What's the matter, asshole? Nothing to say?"

Rich's eyes flashed open. "You fucking bitch!" he yelled.

Kim screamed, throwing the head into the tub. She fled the bathroom and ran downstairs. When she finally stopped screaming, all she could hear was Rich's laughter filling the house.

Shaun Hupp

Chapter Four

Mutilation and Maniacs

Erin stared down at each of her hands. She didn't even recognize them as her hands anymore, or even as hands at all. Hands had fingers. Even a child knew that. What Erin was looking at had no fingers. There were only small nubs where they should have been. Each of the ten nubs ended in horrible blackened burns.

Beyond her hands was the bathroom sink where she had thrown up moments ago. Erin only noticed it again when she heard a plinking sound coming from it. She realized it was her own tears hitting the porcelain that was making that noise.

"Don't cry, my masterpiece," Ben, the Artist, or whatever he wanted to be called, said behind her. "I know it's not great right now, but can't you see the potential?"

Erin shook her head and then quickly stopped. She focused back on where her fingers had been. Even though they were no longer there, she still felt them as if they were. She tried to move her right index finger and swore it moved, even though it was gone like the rest.

"I had to stop the bleeding so cauterizing was necessary. Eventually, it'll heal. Like I said, my work will take a long time. We are far from done."

The smell of burning flesh filled her nostrils once more. Bile rose up in the back of her throat and spewed forth into the sink again. She went to wipe the vomit from her lips with the back of her hand, but couldn't bear to touch her own disfigured flesh.

"Please. No more," Erin said, not wanting to return to that room. It was nice not being tied down.

She felt hands, real hands with fingers on her shoulders. "You don't see my vision. You got only a glimpse. You need to look again. You need to really look."

"No. Please. I can't."

He lifted her upright, but she quickly shut her eyes to avoid the mirror above the sink. She felt his hot breath on her ear. "How many people get to see an artist at work? Most only get to marvel at the completed piece. Few get to see every brushstroke. It is an honor for you. Now, open your eyes."

Erin shook her head, quickly stopping again. "No," she whimpered.

"OPEN YOUR FUCKING EYES!"

Her eyes finally opened as she felt the knife press against her throat.

"I'll admit that my stitching isn't the best, but I'm still learning. Besides, I can always fix them if they fall off."

Erin stared at her face. Earlier, she had only looked at it for a second and heaved into the sink. Now, her stomach was emptied. She wanted to look away from her reflection, but Ben held her upright with a knife to her throat.

"Isn't it beautiful?"

Crude, black lines of thread crisscrossed along her forehead, cheeks, and chin. Each stitch was a pattern crafted by the artist, but they also had a dark purpose. Along the side and bottom of her face, her eight fingers were attached, connected to each other and to Erin. They formed a macabre beard of digits. And on her forehead, her two thumbs jutted out as if they were devil horns.

"Tell me, it's beautiful."

Erin sobbed.

"SAY IT!"

Erin nodded slowly, trying not to shake the fingers sewed to her skin like she had done earlier. With tears in her eyes, she said, "Yes. . . Beautiful."

Gail checked her makeup one last time in the mirror. She wanted everything perfect. She took a step back and smoothed the red, satin dress she bought just for tonight. "Again, I appreciate you coming over like this. It was so last minute, I didn't think I'd be able to find anyone to watch Harper."

"Don't worry about it, Mrs. Griswold. I could really use the money, and it's not like I had any plans."

Amanda wasn't being entirely honest. She did have plans, and they involved her on again, off again boyfriend, Dean. He was upset when she canceled on him, but truth be told, she needed the money. Amanda planned on going to college in the fall, and her family wasn't as well off as Dean's. She already worked two jobs, went to school, and occasionally did some babysitting on the side. Dean had never worked a day in his life and probably wouldn't have to when he went off to college. She hated that about him, but she loved him or at least, she thought she did.

"Well, hopefully, I won't be too late getting back. I mean, it's just a first date. It's just dinner. We don't really know each other that well. I'm not going to do anything too... umm... slutty."

Amanda cracked a smile. Gail was newly divorced and decided to finally jump back into the dating world. It had been awhile, though. She had been with her husband for fifteen years since she was in her mid-twenties. Everything fell apart for her when Gail found out he had been cheating on her. When the dust finally settled, she ended up with the house and her seven-year-old son, Harper.

"If you need me to stay here all night, I will," Amanda said. "I promise not to judge you too much."

Gail laughed, turning a slight shade of red. "Well, I doubt that will happen. I want to take things slow, make sure he's the right guy for me. I don't want to fu... mess things up again."

"Mrs. Griswold. I'm eighteen. You can say fuck in front of me."

Gail's mouth dropped, and Amanda saw she was looking behind her. Amanda turned around and saw Harper coming down the stairs. He already had his Spider-man pajamas on.

"Mom, are you leaving already?"

"Yep. Don't worry, kiddo. Amanda is going to take good care of you," Gail said. She checked her watch. "Crap. I hope there isn't much traffic on the 36. Got to run."

Gail bent down and kissed her son on the cheek. She went to the door, gave them both a wave, and rushed out to her car in the driveway.

"So Harper, I saw there was a Friday the Thirteenth marathon on tonight. . ." Amanda said, turning back to the young boy she was put in charge of.

The boy's eyes lit up. "Can we have popcorn?"

Amanda nodded. "I think it's on channel 126. You save me a spot on the couch, and I'll make the popcorn."

"Deal!" he said, running off to the living room.

Harper was always fascinated with anything scary. Amanda didn't get it. They both knew that kind of stuff would give him nightmares and yet, he kept coming back for more. His mother didn't seem to care, so Amanda let him watch whatever he wanted.

Amanda stepped into the kitchen and went to the cabinet. She could already hear the tv in the other room flipping through channels. Amanda had finally found the popcorn packets when she thought she heard something else. She stopped and tried to focus on the source of the sound. There was a sudden creak nearby.

"Hello? Harper?"

There was the sound again, but Amanda couldn't pinpoint where it was coming from. The kitchen only had two exits. One was the way she just came from, and the other was the mudroom that led to the backyard. She stepped toward the latter. Even if it was nothing, she still wanted to make sure the door was locked.

"Hello?"

She reached the threshold of the doorway and slowly peeked around the corner. There was nothing except for some shoes, a coat closet, and the backdoor. Amanda sighed in relief.

Then, she noticed two things: One, the door wasn't locked, and two, there were fresh, muddy footprints on the tile floor. She turned to run, and the closet burst open. She was grabbed from behind. A hand clamped over her mouth, holding back her screams.

Harper sat with his eyes glued to the horrors on the tv screen and never heard a thing.

"Sounds like you fucked up big time with that one, to be honest."

Alex nodded. "I can't deny that. I was new to the whole killing thing. I did get better, though."

"Yeah? Well, I'll admit it. That tale was pretty entertaining, but I'm still wondering how you went from that guy to this legendary Bay City Slasher."

"It's Bay River Slasher and believe me, it wasn't easy. The cops knew that kill and the several after it were all the work of the same guy. They had to have. There was no one else out there as brutal as I was. I'm sure of it. But you know how it is."

Owen raised an eyebrow.

Big, dumb, and clueless.

"Cops don't like to cause a panic. Besides that, they don't want to look like idiots. They don't want people knowing there's a serial killer on the loose and that they couldn't capture him."

"So, what changed that?"

Alex smiled, looking around to make sure no one else was eavesdropping. "Oh, I'll tell you. If the cops were going to cover up all my kills, I was just going to have to make a public statement myself."

*****

I had played it safe, but at the same time, I wanted to be unpredictable. I didn't want there to be a pattern that the police could pick up on. I never killed another hitchhiker. Instead, I moved on to a prostitute, then a homeless man, then a jogger, and then a drunk. They were all alone, in different parts of the city of Bay River, and none of them saw it coming. In the end, their blood was spilled on the pavement, but always in some dark alleyway. I didn't want to get caught in the middle of my playtime. That just helped the police cover my tracks.

I knew I had to do something about that.

Betty Scottsdale was the answer. She was entirely different from my other kills. She was rich, she was well known, and she was old. There was no pattern to who I killed, only in the vile and twist things I did to them, before and after their deaths. I had plans for Betty. Her death would be the worst yet, and the world would see it.

The world would see me.

The old bat lived in a huge mansion all by herself. At the age of 73, she had already outlived her husband. Rumor had it that he killed himself to get away from her. Regardless, he was gone, and all of the money he made through his investments went to her. She didn't share a single dime with her family and they, in turn, stayed away from her. In fact, she didn't share any money with anyone. That included a security company.

Well past midnight, I broke a back window and entered Betty's home. I still wanted to be careful. I had parked well off the property. I wore a mask even though I was sure there were no cameras. Gloves covered my hands so I wouldn't leave fingerprints on the dust-covered furniture. I felt a little more professional than I had been since my first kill.

Scanning the house with my small pocket flashlight, I quickly found the master bedroom. Betty's snoring could be heard halfway down the hallway, making me rethink the theory of why her husband killed himself. I quietly entered the dark room, tip-toeing to the king-size bed that seemed to swallow her tiny frame. I shined my light on her. Mrs. Scottsdale's mouth hung open while that annoying sound continued. Drool puddled on her floral pillow so much so that I considered drowning her in it.

Unzipping my bag of knives, I decided it was time to get started. "Betty, it's time to wake up."

Her snoring continued unphased.

"Betty? Betty!"

Still, no reaction. Clearly, she had all the money in the world and was too cheap to spring for a hearing aid. I figured if her ears didn't work, why would she need them? I grabbed her left ear with one hand and with the other, began sawing through it with one of my shorter knives. Her eyes finally opened. Her snoring stopped. Her open mouth now had a scream coming from it.

I held the newly detached ear to my mouth and yelled into it, "Can you hear me, Mrs. Scottsdale?"

Betty flung off the blanket and scrambled out of her bed. I watched in horror as she tripped and fell to the floor. I was watching in horror because who would have guessed that this old bitty slept in the nude.

"Oh, come on! No one wants to see that," I said, looking away as her wrinkled, pale ass pointed up in the air. I tossed the ear over my shoulder and went over to her withered frame, trying not to directly look at her.

"Please," she cried. "Take anything you want."

I smiled through the hole in my ski mask. "I plan on it."

Grabbing my bag and her ankle, I dragged her from her bedroom. Her screams didn't stop until we reached the stairs. I chuckled as I heard her head hit each and every step. Then, we went out the front door, and I pulled her limp body across the front lawn.

"Are you going to rape me?"

I stopped dead in my tracks and dropped her ankle. "You've got to be kidd-" I turned back to her and stared in horror at her thin, pale legs. They were covered in spider veins and were spread, revealing a gray tumbleweed of hair between them. She was giving herself to me in exchange for her life. I'm a serial killer. I stab people. I rip their insides out and cover myself in their blood. This, however, was too much for me.

I threw up all over her grass.

From the corner of my eye, I noticed those two pancakes she calls an ass trying to crawl away, and I forced myself to stand up. I had had enough. I pulled out my butcher knife and plunged it into her back. Her skin was so thin and brittle, it offered no resistance. She barely let out a wheeze, and she was gone.

"The shit I do to get famous."

Before me, in her front yard, was a large fountain. It was my destination and a major part of my plan. In the center was a statue of some Roman God or somebody. I wasn't really too sure. Surrounding him were other figures of people and children holding their hands out to the man in the middle.

With all my knives in front of me, I began my work. I carved through Betty's decrepit body and started removing her organs. When I had one out, I tossed it into the fountain. Soon, the water had turned red as her liver, lungs, heart, spleen, and everything else floated among the sculptures. Then, wading through the murky water, I wrapped her intestines around each of the people and connected them to the God in the center. Do you know how much intestines the human body has? Quite a bit from what I found out. There was one last thing the fountain needed. I jumped out of the water and crouched down over Betty's empty body. I took my small carving knife out and sliced away at her face until it peeled off like a slice of bologna. I grabbed my roll of duct tape and headed back in the water. I placed her face over both the God's two faces and taped it there so it would stay.

I started laughing. "You've never looked better, Betty." I had noticed that when I stretched out her flesh, I managed to get rid of all the wrinkles on her face. Seeing my creation, my spirit was so lifted, I leaned in and planted a big kiss right on those severed lips.

Before I left the property, I set a notebook on the edge of the fountain. In it, I had details about my previous kills with information that only I could have known. People were finally going to see me for what I was.

*****

"So, wait a minute," Owen said. "I don't get it. Couldn't the police just hide your notebook like they covered up all the other stuff?"

"Here's the beauty of it: the police weren't the first people on the scene. Right after going over to her house, I contacted every local newspaper I could think of with a written letter. Now, I figured they must have tons of crazy people claiming all sorts of things so I wasn't sure telling them I was a serial killer would work. So, you know what I did?"

Owen shook his head.

"I told them that my name was Betty Scottsdale and at eight AM the following morning, I would be announcing I was giving all my money away. You wouldn't believe how many reporters showed up. They all got way more than they bargained for. They all got their page one headline."

"Don't you even think about it."

Kim jumped as she was about to buckle her seatbelt. Then, she saw it: Her reflection in the rearview mirror. "I'm leaving, and you can't stop me." She buckled herself in and inserted the key in the ignition. She started the car, lighting up her dark driveway.

"No. I can't. But the police, they can. When they find that body and they will, they will come for you."

"But. . . But he just won't stop laughing. I can't take it!"

Her doppelganger smirked in the mirror. "Rich can't hurt you anymore. You took care of him. You just need to finish the job. You're a lot stronger than you give yourself credit for."

"No. I'm not. If I were, I would have left him years ago. Instead, I just took the abuse."

"You slipped up. Everyone does. Now's the time to remember when you were strong and be that person again."

"I can't. I don't remember." Kim could feel the tears rolling down her cheeks, yet her reflection had none.

"I remember. Now, it's time you do too.

*****

"Bitch, where's my money!?"

Kim didn't understand what was happening. One minute she was in her car and the next she was in the apartment she grew up in. Not only that but her mother, as she looked over thirty years ago, was standing in front of the door as it rattled on its hinges.

"Kimmy!" she yelled. "You need to hide, sweetie."

But she couldn't move. Her legs were locked in fear. She looked down at them, and then looked at the rest of her body. She wasn't an adult anymore. She was just a little kid.

"Kimmy! Get out of-"

The door busted open, and two large men barged in, knocking her mother onto the garbage-covered floor. Both had on oversized jackets featuring different basketball teams, sneakers, and plenty of jewelry. One carried a baseball bat. Kim felt warm urine spread down the front of her pants, just as it did all those years ago.

"Please, Ronny. Just give me a little more time. I'm good for it."

"Gave you enough time, you junkie-bitch," the man she assumed was Ronny said. "Now, we are here to collect."

"I don't have it, I swear, but I can get it next week."

Ronny shook his head. "What do you think, Eddy?"

Eddy smiled. "I say we give her a break. We can wait until next week."

Kim was relieved, and it looked like her mother was too. All she wanted was for these men to leave. Then, she'd hug her mom and tell her everything was going to be okay.

Ronny nodded. "Next week, but today, we collect our interest."

The men reached down and grabbed Kim's mom. They flipped her onto her stomach, holding her against the carpet. Kim watched in horror as Eddy ripped her skirt away. Her mother kicked at him, but a slap to the face from Ronny knocked the fight out of her.

"Bitch, don't make this harder for you than it's going to be."

"Please," she cried. "I'll do whatever you want. Just let my daughter go in the other room. Don't let her see this."

Ronny turned back to Kim. He smiled and gave her a little wave. "I don't think so," he said, while never taking his eyes off Kim. "In fact, I think this will be a fitting punishment for you, Mags. Your daughter should have to watch what happens when you cross somebody like me. Call it a life lesson. Now, if she so much as blinks, so much as takes her eyes off us for one second, we will fucking kill you. Your life is in your daughter's hands."

Kim stared at her mother. She looked broken and defeated. Kim hoped whatever they had planned was over quickly for both their sakes.

"Kimmy, sweetie. Just do what the man says okay. Mommy will be okay. Don't worry. I just need you to be brave. Can you do that for me?"

Kim nodded, and Eddy ripped her mother's underwear off. Both men dropped their pants and had a hand on their privates. Each rubbed it back and forth. Kim had seen a penis before but never like Ronny's. It didn't hang limp but was sticking straight out.

"Ah, shit!" Eddy yelled out.

"What?" Ronny asked.

"I fucking drank too much. My dick ain't getting hard. I wish I knew we were doing this. I would've cut back."

"I have an idea," Ronny said with a laugh. "Why not use that long, hard thing in your other hand?"

Eddy held up the baseball bat. "Good idea. That's why you're the boss, boss."

Kim shook her head and went to close her eyes. Her mother stared at her, giving her a look that seemed to beg her to hold on. Then, that look turned into a grimace, just before, she screamed. Kim looked up and saw that Eddy was pushing the top end of the bat into her mom. She cried out again as it slid in another inch.

"Going in dry. I fucking love it. Swing batter, batter. Swing!"

Ronny grabbed Kim's mom by the hair and pulled her head back. Suddenly, he thrust his penis into her mouth. "If I feel teeth, I'll knock them out," he said as he held her face against his groin.

She gagged, tears and black eye shadow streamed down her face. Saliva poured from her mouth as Ronny pulled out, then thrust himself back in repeatedly hitting the back of her throat each time. Her cries were muffled as the baseball bat in her vagina was also pulled out only to be pushed back in again over and over.

Kim covered her ears so that she didn't have to hear her mom's gurgled cries. She didn't dare close her eyes. All she could do was stare at the men as they violated her mom. When they were finally done, they left her crying on the floor, laying in a puddle that was a mixture of semen, saliva, and blood from her vagina.

As Ronny was about to shut the door, he turned back to them. "Next week. If you don't have my money then, we won't go so easy on you. Maybe, we'll teach your pretty little daughter how to suck dick."

The door slammed, not fully closing since it was broken, and Kim ran to her mother. Kim held her tight as she shook, staring up at her from the floor.

"You were so brave. You were so brave. . ."

*****

"You were so brave," her reflection in the rearview mirror said.

"I. . . I haven't thought about that in years."

"You repressed it. You buried it deep down inside your mind, hoping it would never come to light. The problem is that when you did that, you created me. I'm the version of you that remembers all the awful shit you went through. If you hadn't done away with me, you probably would have killed Rich years ago. Instead, you hid from your memories. You hid from me, but I found you."

Kim looked over her shoulder at the front door of her house. She still wasn't sure she could go back in there. Nevertheless, Kim knew she had to.

"You tried so hard, but in the end, you need me, Kim. If we're going to get through this, we need to work as a team."

Chapter Five

Making the Maniacs

"We're working so well together. I can't wait to see you when I have you fully complete."

Erin pulled on the cords that were tied to each hand yet again, attached to two of the bedposts, keeping her on the bloody mattress. Even without fingers and thumbs, the cords were tied tight enough around her wrists that there was no give. Her feet were retied in a similar matter, but more secure. She gave up struggling for now.

"Please. Let me go. I'm not your perfect canvas. I'm not your masterpiece. I'm just a senior in high school. I shouldn't be here. I want to be with my family."

Ben shook his head. "I'm afraid that's quite impossible. This art is bigger than the both of us. We can't stop now. This is why I wanted you to look at yourself in the mirror."

"I look horrible. You turned me into a monster!"

"In a sense, yes. The Devil is a very unique individual. Tragic even. Maybe when we finish the next part of the canvas, you'll understand more."

"No. Please," Erin begged. The fingers attached to her face shook as her body trembled at the thought of more mutilations. "I think I'm done. I'm a masterpiece already. Really, I am."

Her captor paid no attention to her and went back to his tray of knives at the foot of the bed. From there, he grabbed a hacksaw and returned to her. "The Devil usually has his beard and his horns. That part is complete. Another aspect of his physiology is his cloven hooves." He carefully lowered the blade between her second and third toe.

"NO!" Erin screamed, trying to kick at him. It was no use. The cords not only had her feet tied to the bedposts but to each other as well, giving her no slack.

Ben pushed the hacksaw forward, cutting through the flesh between her toes. Erin cried out as the pain shot through her leg. The blade pulled back, cutting even deeper, hitting bone. Erin bit her lip as the blade sawed forward again. She tried to focus on the taste of blood in her mouth. Back and forth, the saw continued while her captor grunted with each motion.

"Shit."

Erin looked at him, trying to avoid looking at her foot. Ben held up the hacksaw. Its thin blade hung in two pieces.

"I guess these things aren't strong enough for the bones in your feet. I can't believe I was so stupid. DAMNIT!"

He flung the broken tool off into the corner of the room. He grabbed the tray of knives and flipped them onto the floor in a rage. Erin breathed a sigh of relief as Ben stormed off, leaving the room. She finally looked at her foot. The gash between her toes looked nasty but was only about a half an inch. Erin closed her eyes and licked the blood from her lips.

Try to calm down. Maybe he's done for the day. Maybe he'll be so upset with his failure that he'll stop. Maybe he'll let me go and I can-

A loud grinding noise filled the basement room. Erin's eyes flashed open to see Ben standing over her feet. He had returned with an electrical circular saw in his hands.

"This should do nicely," he said, returning the saw to the spot he was working on earlier. Erin's mouth hung open in shock, but no sound came forth. The spinning blade sliced through her skin and bone quickly, spattering blood across her thighs. Finally, Erin screamed and didn't stop until the saw powered down.

"All done. You can look now."

Erin shook her head, keeping her eyes closed.

"Don't make me cut off your eyelids. Look at your foot!"

Erin reluctantly opened her eyes. It was hard to see through the tears. She blinked several times until she saw Ben's eye staring at her between the two flaps that used to be her foot. The saw had cut through several inches of bone, almost to her ankle, leaving her with a V-shaped appendage.

"Do you like it?"

Erin felt woozy. The room seemed to spin. She felt the room getting dimmer before her body finally gave in to the darkness. The last thing she had remembered before she passed out was the words: "Sleep now, my canvas. When you awake, we'll do the other foot."

Amanda struggled against the man's grip. Seeing no other option, she bit down on the hand covering her mouth. The man yelped and let go of her. She quickly spun around, raising her fist ready to attack.

"Stop. Stop. Stop! It's me."

Amanda lowered her hand. "You fucking idiot! You scared the shit out of me."

Her boyfriend Dean rubbed his hand where her teeth mark embedded in his skin. "Sorry. You didn't have to bite my hand off, though."

"What do you want, Dean? This is crazy. What was so important you had to break into a house to see me?"

"I missed you.'

Amanda rolled her eyes.

"I'm serious. It seems like we haven't seen each other all week. We were supposed to go out tonight and then, you canceled. I thought maybe we could still hang out, you know, while you work."

"Dean, you should really go. If Harper sees you, he'll tell his mom and then, I'll be out of a job."

"Then, send the brat to bed."

Amanda flinched at the cruelty of his words. Harper was a good kid. A little morbid, but good. "You need to go. I will see you on Mon-"

Before she could finish her sentence, he was on her. His body pressed up to hers, forcing her against the wall of the mudroom. She tried to push him away, but his lips found hers. His tongue pushed into her mouth. As the fight in her left, she felt his hands move to her breasts. Her nipples grew hard through the fabric of her shirt.

Damnit, girl. You always fall for this shit.

Amanda found herself kissing Dean back. Her hands stopped pushing him away and now, held him close, pressing his groin against hers. His mouth moved down her neck, and a moan escaped her lips. She felt herself getting wet.

"Dean?"

He kept kissing and sucking on her neck.

"Dean, did you bring condoms?"

He pulled his face away from her body and smirked. "Of course, babe."

Amanda blushed. "Fine. You stay right here, and I'll take Harper up to his room."

He nodded and smacked her ass as she left the room. Amanda saw Harper's brown mop of hair poking out from the top of the back of the couch. On the television mounted on the wall, blood and gore flew across the screen accompanied by screeching horror music. "Sorry, buddy. I forgot that your mom said she wanted you in bed early tonight. Said you had been staying up too late and needed to get back on track for school.

Somewhat of a lie. It was kind of true.

"Awww! Do I have to?" he whined.

"Yeppers. Come on." She took his hand and led him upstairs. The door to his room had planet stickers all over it and a 'No Girls Allowed' sign. Harper always made an exception for her. He climbed into bed and pulled the covers over himself.

"Goodnight, Harper."

"Wait! Amanda. . . Can you check the closet?"

She sighed and shook her head. "Harper, we've been over this. You're getting too old to believe in monsters. That stuff on the TV is fake: Rubber suits and CGI."

"Okay," he quietly said, still sounding unsure.

Wanting to get back to Dean, she said, "Well, sleep tight, and when you wake up, your mom will be home. I'll probably see you in a week if she needs me again."

"Okay. Night."

Harper watched as Amanda left his room, shutting the door behind him. Light from the street lamps outside allowed him to see a little, letting him feel somewhat safe. He was bummed that he couldn't stay up to watch his movie, but he had already seen it a dozen times.

He was about to close his eyes when there was a sudden creak from the corner of the room. It was the closet. The door opened slightly. Harper threw the covers over his head and made sure his feet were under too.

"There's no such thing as monsters. There's no such thing as monsters. There's no. . ."

If Harper were looking, he would have seen the meat cleaver emerge from the darkness of the closet.

"So, what happened? Why did you stop killing?"

Alex took a sip from his drink. "I had my fame, but the public demanded that I be caught. They had police officers and detectives working nonstop. All they needed was for me to make a mistake. And I did."

"What'd you do?"

"I got sloppy. They got a partial print off a tranny I hacked to death in a parking garage. Luckily I didn't have my fingerprints on file. The cops let the newspapers report everything they found just to help with the mass hysteria. The media told the public they were close to capturing me. Another crime scene had my blood from when a cab driver fought back. Another murder got the model of my car and possible colors from a gas station's black and white security camera. Hell after that, I didn't even want to take my car out on the road to go to my job. My paranoia was growing faster than my urges. I was done."

"You were done? No more Bay River Slasher?"

"Not quite. I managed to suppress my urges for a bit. If they came up, I had plenty of images from past kills I could focus on. It worked. I thought I had beat it. I hadn't killed in over two years. Then, I saw her. . ."

"Oh, I've got to hear about this."

*****

I had moved to a new state. I had changed locations before to throw off the police, but this move had another purpose. Instead of a new city, this was more of a small town. I figured with fewer people there would be less temptation. The nationwide manhunt for me was over. I had successfully disappeared, and the police tried to sweep everything under the rug. They claimed that serial killers don't just stop. I probably attacked the wrong person, and my body would turn up one day.

I eased myself into a boring, normal life. I was out grocery shopping one day when I saw her. I had never seen her before, and I thought I knew everyone in that small community. Her long blond hair danced with every graceful movement from her. Her skin was tan and flawless. She looked a few years older than me, but her body was kept in perfect shape.

I felt those urges coming back. Old habits nagged at me, and I began to tail her through the store like I would have years ago. She went to one of the checkout lanes, and I went to the next one over. She walked out to her car, and I walked to mine. She pulled out of her parking spot, and seconds later, I began my pursuit. I followed her back to a modest two-story house on the other side of town. She and either a boyfriend or husband unloaded their groceries while I sat halfway down the street.

What are you doing? You need to leave.

I should have, but I couldn't. I had to force myself. Finally, after about an hour of internal debate, I threw the car in drive and left. I planned to never return, I swear. That night the urges came to me again in the form of dreams. I fantasized about everything I wanted to do to her. In the morning, the images wouldn't stop flashing before my eyes. I drove back to her house and watched it for hours. I learned her and her husband's patterns. I told myself I had to stop. I didn't listen. After several days, I had a plan.

Early in the morning, after her husband went to work, I broke into her house. She was watching TV, drinking a cup of coffee, while I snuck up on her. My black, leather bag hung over my shoulder. The weight of it felt good. It was like an old friend I hadn't seen in awhile. I couldn't wait to reminisce.

I grabbed her from behind, cupping one hand over her mouth. The houses were too close together in this suburb. Any kind of scream would draw unwanted attention. Little did I realize that she didn't need to scream for help. She knew how to handle herself.

Her elbow caught me in the gut causing my grip to release for a split second. That was all she needed to twist my arm, brace herself into a lower position, and flip me over her shoulder. My body crashed into her glass coffee table, shattering it. I scrambled away, noticing all the blood on the living room floor.

My blood.

Shit.

My intended victim stood with her fists raised in a boxing stance. While I was watching the house, I had paid no attention to where she went. Clearly, she took some sort of self-defense or exercise class. I hadn't killed in years and had let myself go. I was no match for her. I had to get to my bag of knives that was still behind the couch.

"You messed with the wrong woman, asshole."

"I can see that," I said, trying to sound tough, but it came out as more of a wheeze.

I am fucked.

"My husband will be home any minute. . . Not that I need him."

"No, he won't," I said, finally catching my breath. "He won't be back for hours. That leaves me hours to play with you."

"So, you planned on raping me."

"Not quite."

I lunged for her, going high. She easily countered my attack, throwing me over her shoulder again. My back hit the floor hard. My head, however, hit my bag of knives as she had flipped me over the couch, like I hoped for. I knew I was no match for her, but I could outsmart her. I quickly unzipped it and reached inside, letting my instincts guide me. Out came my butcher knife. I blew some dust off it like someone trying to entice a lover.

I felt a hand grip my hair. I looked up just in time to see a lamp coming toward me. I could have defended myself, but instead, I drove my knife into my attacker's gut. I took the blow to the head, knowing I had done more damage to her. She disappeared in front of the sofa, and I fell to the floor on the other side. I fought desperately to remain conscious. The last thing I needed was to pass out and have the husband/boyfriend come home to find me.

Luckily, I succeed and managed to get back on my feet. She, however, wasn't so lucky. It looked as if she had somehow crawled through the broken glass, trying to get to her cell phone that was across the room on the floor. Her hand was inches from it but never made it. I breathed a sigh of relief. The cell phone must have been on the table when I crashed through it. Had I landed any other way, perhaps the phone would have fallen closer to her.

I was lucky in that aspect, but not so lucky in the fact that I had waited years for this kill and she was already dead. I wanted to hear her beg for her life. I wanted to see the terror in her eyes as I began to slice through her flesh. I was denied my glorious return.

No. I will not be denied my fun.

If I couldn't play with her while she was alive, I would just have to use her lifeless body. I grabbed my bag and opened it up completely, exposing all my long lost friends. Over the next several hours, I used each and every blade to hack away at her body. Nothing was safe. Her fingers. Her toes. My friends did away with them all. When they couldn't cut through the bones of her arms and legs. I found a hammer in the house and used it to smash them. Then, my knives could return to their work. I wouldn't have felt better even if I had my hand on my cock. Eventually, that euphoria returned to me, and I lost myself in my fun. When I finally came to, I stared at what I had done in awe. Inside the fireplace, I had removed the standard wooden logs and replaced them with her naked torso, digits, and limbs. On the mantle above sat her head. Her eyes were wide. Her mouth hung open in a silent scream.

I smiled at her, as I packed up my friends one last time. "Thanks, babe. I really needed that."

*****

"And that was the last time I killed."

Owen set his drink down but didn't take his eyes off his empty glass. "Why don't you finish the story?"

Alex was confused. "There's not much else to tell. I had an extra pair of clothes in my bag so no one would see me covered in blood. I walked-"

"Finish the story."

"What the hell do you want to hear?" Alex asked, getting frustrated. "I had to move once again because I knew they would eventually piece it together with my blood at the crime scene."

"Finish the story," he said, finally taking his eyes off his glass. They stared Alex down.

"I'm not sure what you mean, and now, you're starting to piss me off."

Alex went to stand up, bracing his hands on the bar. Hours of drinking had made his head spin when he tried to get to his feet. Owen's thick hand quickly slapped down on his, squeezing it tight. His eyes told Alex to sit back down. He listened.

"Finish the story," he repeated. "Tell me about the little boy that came down the stairs to see his mother's body in pieces. Tell me about how his father came home hours later and found his son in the middle of living room floor trying desperately to put her body back together. Tell me about how he laid there covered in her blood, staring up at the mantle because he couldn't reach her head."

Alex tried to pull his hand away, but Owen gripped it tighter.

"No. You don't know anything about her son, so let me tell you about myself."

"I was just a kid," Kim said. "A lot has changed since then."

"I know, but you don't seem to understand yet," her reflection in the rearview mirror said. "When your mother was raped, a seed was planted in your head. It grew into me."

"But how does that help me now?"

"I helped you in the past. Don't you remember?"

"No. I. . . No. You don't mean when I-"

"Yes. I helped you survive then, and I can do it again. First, I need you to remember.

*****

Kim was no longer sitting in her car. Instead, she was sitting on a small bed. She looked up and realized she was in her old college dorm room. Posters and notes hung all over the walls. Stacks of papers and books covered her desk. Sunlight poured through the window. A flood of memories filled her head as everything came back to her. She felt the need to finish up some homework before her next class. She thought about her plans for the weekend. Then, she realized what was about to happen that day.

"No. . . Not today."

There was a knock on the door. Kim instinctively asked, "Who is it?" as she stood up and walked toward the door.

No! Don't open the door. Call campus security.

"It's building maintenance," a muffled voice said. "We're checking for Radon."

That's a lie! Don't-

Kim opened the door and was quickly tackled to the floor. A man in a ski mask covered her mouth while two more masked men came inside, locking the door behind them. They looked around the small dorm room and then, shut the blinds.

"Don't scream," the man, holding her down said. He held up a pocket knife. "If you scream, we will hurt you. We don't want to hurt you. Do you understand?"

Kim nodded her head. Then, she watched in horror as the other men began to strip.

"I'm gonna get me some of that tight snatch."

"I get plenty of pussy as it is. I want her ass."

The man on top of her moved off her but left his hand over her mouth. Using his knife, he started cutting away at her clothes. The other men joined in by ripping away the cut sections. With a single cut in the center, her bra came apart. Both men's meaty hands quickly found her breasts.

"Goddamn! I knew these things were going to be worth it."

One of the men leaned forward and placed his mouth on her nipple. Kim's body betrayed her as her nipple stiffened as he sucked and squeezed it.

"Bitch is into it," he said, pulling his mouth away from her breast. "She's totally into it."

A tear rolled down her cheek as the other man pulled her panties off. She bit down on the inside of her lip as she felt a finger slide into her. She closed her eyes and tried to think of something else. It didn't work.

"Flip her over. I want that fucking ass. I'm going in dry too."

Those words.

She remembered all those years ago when those words were spoken to her mother. She remembered her mother being violated. She remembered her standing there, unable to do anything because she was a child.

I'm not a child anymore. I will not be a victim.

Kim bit down on the hand on her mouth and didn't let go. The man screamed out and brought the knife to her face. A well-placed kick to the groin caused him to drop the blade onto her chest. She quickly grabbed it and drove it into the side of his neck. His body fell to the floor as the other men jumped up. They both rushed her but retreated as the knife slashed at their hands. She lunged forward, stabbing one in the shoulder. The other man ran to the door, trying to open it, but forgot to unlock it. By the time he figured that out, Kim was on him. The blade moved in and out of the small of his back several times before he fell limp in front of the door. His bladder and bowels spilled forth onto the floor beneath him. With the door now blocked, Kim turned around to face the man she had stabbed in the shoulder. He knew he was trapped too, so he tried to take the knife. Kim caught him with a kick to his balls. He went down and held his crotch. With no hands free to defend himself, Kim descended on him with stabbing blows. After awhile, he stopped moving.

Kim did not.

"I am not a victim."

*****

"I helped you kill those three men before they could rape you."

"Fine," Kim said to her doppelganger in the mirror. "You helped me, but I didn't like the person I became."

"You survived, though."

"I almost went to prison."

"Maybe stabbing those men over twenty times each after they were already dead was a bit excessive, but the self-defense claim worked."

"And what about cutting their penises off!?"

"Again, the jury saw you as the victim," her reflection said. "They saw a woman that snapped after she was almost raped. You got off with a short psychiatric stay. I would call that a win for you. . . for us."

Kim was quiet.

"So, are you ready to go back inside now? We really need to take care of that body."

Kim looked at herself in the mirror and slowly nodded, turning off the car and opening the door.

Chapter Six

Killing with Knives

Erin awoke. She had lost count of the number of times she passed out because of the agony. She tried to focus her blurry vision on her feet where the pain was. When her sight finally cleared, she let out a scream. The two V-shaped feet stared back her. She didn't want to believe they were hers. It was impossible, but when she moved her legs, Erin saw those deformed hooves move too. They were still tightly bound to the bed as were her hands which barely resembled hands.

"Oh, good. You're up."

Ben entered the room through the door in front of the bed. He placed something on the silver tray with his knives. It looked like a bloody rag, but it hit the platter with a hard thump.

"Are you ready for the next part of your transformation?"

"No. I can't." she cried, shaking her head, feeling her fingers wobble on her chin and cheeks.

"I understand. It can be scary: what's happening to your body. You have to trust me. You're so close to being a masterpiece."

"SOMEONE PLEASE HELP ME!"

Ben sighed. "I told you. No one can hear you through these walls. They were specially built that way. I can see you don't trust me yet, so we're just going to have to move on."

He lifted the bloody rag so that only he could see what was underneath. "I've been studying the Devil for a while now. The beard, the horns, the cloven hooves, they are all part of your transformation, but there is one last part that is very important. Do you know what it is?"

Erin couldn't bring herself to speak. She tried to move her arms and legs in vain. She didn't want to know what he had in mind for her next, but she couldn't look away.

"Forget about the tail and pitchfork. Witches and women alike have all made claims to having the Devil visit them at night to fornicate with them. Sometimes they were willing. A lot of the time they were not. Regardless, they all spoke of what the Devil's penis looked like."

Ben let the rag drop and held up his creation. "His penis was said to be forked like a serpent's tongue, giving it almost a double-sided dildo look. It was described as half-flesh and half-iron. Luckily, I'm pretty good with welding. From what I've been reading, the metal end was inserted into the rectum while the actual penis was put into the vagina to spread his seed during sex."

He carried the V-shaped creation that reminded Erin of her feet toward her. He laid it on her chest between her breasts. "Isn't it beautiful?"

Bile rose up in the back of her throat as the head of the severed penis faced her, blood dripping from the tip. The metal side spiraled upward into a sharp point. She was about to throw up when she saw Ben bend over and reach under the bed. His hand emerged holding the needle and thread he had used to reattach her fingers. Now, instead of vomit, it was another scream that sat at the back of her throat.

"Don't worry. I'll attach it in front of your vagina. I believe the Devil would have it that way too. With a penis, a vagina, and breasts, you can seduce either gender!"

The scream came forth when he grabbed the penis and placed it against her red pubic hair.

Ben smiled, waiting for her to stop. When she finally did, he said, "I thought you'd recognize it. Guess not. Earlier you asked what happened to Jake. I'm afraid I not only killed him, but I used him for parts."

Amanda grasped his penis. Dean moaned as she started to slowly stroke him with her hand down the front of his basketball shorts. He was already hard and ready for her.

"Not yet."

"What?" Dean lifted his head up from where it was buried in her neck.

She slid her hand out of his pants and playfully pushed him off her. "I have to go check on Harper. I want to make sure he's asleep. We wouldn't want him coming down here and seeing all the stuff we're going to be doing. Might warp his little mind. . . even more so."

She tried to get up, but Dean pulled her back down on top of him. "I'm sure he's fine. Now, tell me more about these mind-warping things."

Amanda kissed him deeply, slipping her tongue into his mouth. Then, she jumped back up. "I'll let you decide on the specifics, but first, I need to check on Harper."

She took off before Dean could grab her again. She made it halfway up the stairs before she heard him say, "You are so sucking my dick."

Slowly and quietly pushing open Harper's No Girls Allowed door, Amanda tip-toed into his room, going up to his bed to check on him. The blanket covered his entire body, even his head. Amanda wasn't surprised. He did that when he got scared, which was often because of the movies he watched.

"Harper," she whispered. "Are you still awake?"

Nothing. She smiled, thinking about all the things she wanted to do with Dean, then Amanda saw a dark stain on the blanket. It had been a long time since Harper had peed the bed, but this was odd. It was higher up, more toward his head. She thought that maybe he threw up, but he didn't seem sick earlier. Carefully, she lifted the blanket up and pulled it down.

Harper's face was gone. A small, grinning skull with brown hair and eyeballs was all that remained of his head.

Amanda opened her mouth to scream, but a gloved hand clamped over her jaw. Before she knew what was happening, the blade of a meat cleaver was inserted between her teeth, slicing through the skin of her cheeks. The man's hand left the handle of the knife and gripped the top of her head. She felt the man pushing down on the top of her head and up on her jaw at the same time. Her upper and lower sets of teeth pressed hard against both sides of the cleaver. The pressure increased, and Amanda's muffled cries were drowned out by the sound of her teeth cracking. She tried to kick at the massive body behind her, but it was no use. The teeth that didn't shatter inside her mouth drove up into her gums. Amanda gagged on the blood as it poured down her throat and came out her nose. She couldn't breathe anymore. The man didn't stop. She clawed at his arms, scratching his skin, but he never flinched. Finally, she fell limp as she felt the fight drain out of her. Amanda's body was tossed onto the bed next to Harper's. The last thing she saw before her life ended was the face of the giant looking down on her. It was a crudely stretched and torn version of Harper's face. Evil eyes stared down at her through the holes where Harper's should have been.

"What do you want from me?"

"For now, I just want you to listen," Owen said, finally releasing his grip on Alex's hand. "I listened to your stories. How about mine?"

"Fine. Tell me." Alex knew he didn't have a choice.

*****

Some people have memories as early as two or three. Not me. My earliest memories are from that day when I was five. I walked down those stairs to the sight of blood behind and in front of the couch. The glass, living room table was smashed. I couldn't understand what was going on.

Then, I saw my mother's head over the fireplace.

Again, I didn't understand. "Mommy, where's your body? Are you hiding?"

No answer.

"Mommy, why aren't you talking? Are we playing?"

No answer.

I went to the fireplace and then, noticed the arms and legs inside it. I opened the glass, which normally had a safety lock on it, but it was left undone. I started carrying every limb, finger, toe, etc. and placed them in the area of the living room floor not covered in glass and blood. I remember later in life being good with puzzles, so I must have been good at them at that time as well. My small, bloody hands began to piece my mother's body together. When I finally had all but one piece, I went back to the fireplace.

"Mommy, I put you back together. I just need your head."

No answer.

I jumped over and over again but was unable to reach her. Frustrated, I started to cry. "Mommy, I can't do it!"

I went back to what was left of her body and curled up next to it. I wrapped several pieces of hand and arm around my body and laid there crying until my father returned. My eyes never left my mother's.

*****

"Would it help if I said I was sorry?" Alex had no idea what to say. He just hoped to get out of that bar with his life.

Owen shook his head. "Nothing you could ever say or do could bring her back."

"So, what do we do now?"

"For now, you listen to the rest of my story. Maybe then you'll understand what kind of monster you made me."

"So, first you kill me. Now, you're going to dismember my body. HA! You still believe that I'm the monster here?"

Kim stared down at the severed head of her abusive husband that lie on his own chest. Blood from his neck stump slowly circled the drain in the bathtub. "Yes. You did this." She looked at her reflection in the silver faucet. Her doppelganger nodded with approval.

Rich laughed. "I'll admit that I might have had it coming, but you have had this part of you all along. You have always been a monster. I just awakened it."

Kim tried to ignore him as she put the teeth of the hacksaw into the crease of his elbow. It tore through his flesh. She felt queasy, seeing the muscle and skin pull away from the bone. She had had enough blood for one day.

"This time a judge won't see you as a victim. You could have left me. You could have filed for divorce. Instead, you did this. You're a cold-blooded killer. Look at you. You're trying to hide the body like a criminal."

"Don't listen to him," her reflection said. "He's going to try to trick you. You can't let him."

Kim dropped the hacksaw onto the tile floor. "He's right. I can't fix this."

"Now, call the police," the severed head said. "Tell them what happened and maybe you can get a temporary insanity plea. You're just a housewife that snapped."

Kim stood up and started to leave. Her reflection in the bathroom mirror stopped her. "No. You might not be strong enough, but I am. Let me have control, and I can take care of this. Remember, I've helped you before."

She's right. Rich is trying to trick me. I need to let. . . her handle it.

"Good girl."

Kim turned around as if she was on autopilot and headed back to the tub. Rich started to say something, but Kim quickly grabbed his head and smashed it over and over against the edge of the porcelain tub. She held the head up. Its nose was crushed. Any teeth that remained in his mouth were jagged shards.

"YOU BITCH!"

Opening his lips, she shoved the faucet down his throat. Rich gagged, his words now muffled. Kim grabbed the fallen hacksaw and went back to work. She closed her eyes, but could still feel everything that was taking place. She tried to think of happier times, trying to ignore the sounds of limbs being cut, bones being smashed against the tub, and the feeling of blood flowing through her fingers. She tried to think of how much better her life would be without Rich. She felt herself opening up garbage bags and throwing pieces of Rich inside. Kim's hands felt hair, and she pulled the head off the faucet.

"You'll never get away with this. They'll catch you."

His taunts continued but were quieted by the inside of the garbage bag. Kim continued to think happy thoughts. She finally opened her eyes when she felt the hot spray of the shower strike her face. Looking down, she saw the blood being rinsed off her body.

There's so much of it.

"Don't worry," her reflection in the faucet said. "Just finish cleaning yourself up, and we're almost done."

Kim listened, finishing her shower. She stepped out onto the tile and grabbed a towel to dry off. She carefully avoided all the four garbage bags, making her way to the mirror. She wasn't sure what to do next.

"Okay, first things first," her reflection said. "You need to get some new clothes on. I had to throw your old clothes out."

Kim nodded, looking down at her own nudity. All the blood was gone. She was clean. She felt brand new. Her husband was gone. She was finally free. Not wanting to lose this feeling, she knew she could finish whatever needed to be done.

"Next, we need to hide those trash bags somewhere in the house where no one will ever find them. If you try to hide them somewhere outside this house, someone could find it. The police would figure out whose body that is and they would come looking for you. You need to keep him here and live out the rest of your life in this house."

Rich's muffled laugh could be heard from one of the garbage bags.

"Don't worry, Kim. We'll put him somewhere where you can't hear him. You'll never have to listen to that laugh again.'

"But where? Where in the house can I put him?"

"Do you remember when Rich was doing those renovations in the basement and he forgot to nail down all those wooden panels by the furnace? You can easily throw those garbage bags back there and pound in a few nails. No one would ever look there."

It made perfect sense. There was plenty of room in that space. Rich was just too lazy to finish his projects. But there was one problem. . .

"Yes. You'll have to wait for your tenant to go out for a bit before you use your key to let yourself in. He keeps to himself, but you know he usually goes out for a bit at night. That's your window. Bring the trash bags, hammer, and nails. You'll be done in ten minutes. Ben will never know you were there."

Chapter Seven

Murdering with Maniacs

"Beautiful, isn't it?"

Erin didn't want to look, but she knew he would make her if she didn't. She looked between her legs where she felt the weight of both cold iron and the softness of dead, wilted flesh. Black stitches crisscrossed her groin area much like they did on her face. She shuddered as she saw that very thread connecting her boyfriend's penis to the sensitive skin near her vagina. It lay for the most part flaccid except for the circle of metal at the base that connected it to the other penis below it. The fake iron shaft was not limp. It stood fully erect, its welded 8-inch frame spiraled to a sharp point at the tip.

Erin began to cry. Ben looked confused. "You should be happy. You're a masterpiece."

She couldn't take anymore. She had no idea what he had planned for her after she was complete, but she figured it wasn't good. He had mentioned earlier that he planned on killing her eventually. She wished he had. "I. . . I am. These are tears of joy."

"Marvelous!" He clapped his hands.

"It's just. . ."

"Just what?"

"I'm very hungry."

"Oh, where are my manners? I've barely fed you anything. I'll see what's in the fridge."

"No. I thought maybe we could celebrate my. . . completion. Maybe you could go out and bring back something fancy. Maybe even some wine."

Ben smiled. "I like the way you think. I'll be right back, and we'll celebrate."

Erin didn't expect what came next. Ben leaned down and kissed her. She had to fight back the urge to vomit as his tongue entered her mouth and a hand found her breast. She didn't want to give him any reason to suspect she was lying about being happy, so she kissed him back. She flinched as she felt the threads being pulled on her cheek. She realized that he was running his other hand through her beard. His fingers intertwined with hers. She felt the bile at the back of her throat as his lips moved away from hers and his tongue traced a line down from her mouth to the fingers. He began to suck on the fingers attached to her. Then, he playfully nibbled on one of her fingernails. Erin stared in horror as she saw the hand that was on her breast slowly inch its way down her stomach and wrap around Jake's penis. He began to stroke the severed member while blood dripped its head.

"Please. Ben. There's plenty of time for all this. We should eat first. We need our strength. . . for later."

He pulled his mouth away, letting the finger slip from his lips. Saliva flicked across her chest. "You're right. First, we'll eat. Then, we'll have the rest of the night. Just you and me."

Erin swallowed and forced herself to say, "I can't wait."

"I'm tired of waiting," Dean said, standing up from the couch. He was thinking of all the things he wanted to do to Amanda, but as long as she had been upstairs, he had lost his erection. "This is bullshit."

Now all he could think about was leaving and going over to Angela Miller's house. He had been seeing her behind Amanda's back, and truth be told, he enjoyed spending time with her more. She was on the pill. Dean didn't have to wear a condom like he had to with his girlfriend. Amanda might talk about doing all sorts of wild things, but that's all it was: talk. Angela did anything he wanted and let him put his cock wherever he wanted.

If she tells me I have to leave, it's over.

Dean headed up the stairs and went to Harper's room. The door was wide open, but he didn't see either of them.

"Amanda?" he whispered. "Are you in here?"

He walked into the bedroom, looking all around. He still didn't see either of them. There was a blanket-covered lump in the center of the bed. Dean assumed it was Harper. He leaned over the bed and grabbed hold of the blanket. Then, he decided against it, worrying that he might wake the kid.

I wonder if she's getting ready in the master bedroom. It would be nice to fuck on a real bed for once and not a couch or in the back of my car.

Dean turned around to leave, hoping he'd find Amanda. Out of the shadows, a large figure emerged. Dean backed away and fell onto the bed, onto the lump under the covers. It felt wet against his back. The man stepped into the light, letting Dean get a look at the meat cleaver in his hand. He also got to see the man's face or rather, what was covering his face. On his head was a strange amalgamation of Amanda and Harper's faces: child and babysitter, their flesh intertangled together in an unholy union. Underneath the mask of merged skin, was the face of a madman. He advanced toward Dean. The teen panicked and rolled off the bed, bringing the blanket with him. He quickly stood back up and stared in horror at what lie beneath. His girlfriend and Harper were next to each other. Each of their faces was a gory mess of blood and bone.

Dean looked back to his attacker just in time to see the cleaver come down. He jumped backward, dodging the killing blow. Seeing no other option behind him or to the left, he went back to the right, hopping back onto the bed, and leaping over the bodies. In midair, a gloved hand grabbed onto his ankle, pulling him back. Dean screamed and fell face-first on top of Amanda and Harper. His open mouth landed directly onto Amanda's, giving her one final kiss before the meat cleaver slammed down into the back of his head.

Alex brought his drink to his lips and downed it in one gulp. He wished he was anywhere but here. Looking up at the television screen, he saw the chaos from the terrorist attack in Spain. The television had been re-airing it over and over again, forcing the world to pay attention to the act of violence. The terrorists had the world hostage via the media since yesterday. Alex wished he was in that building when the bomb went off. At least he might be able to get a quick death from the explosion. His drinking buddy didn't seem like the type to get things over and done with.

"You could at least pay attention to me when I speak."

"Sorry," Alex said, taking his eyes off the lives lost and building ruins on the tv and returning them to the man whose life he ruined.

"Now, where was I?"

*****

I grew up not only without a mother but a father as well. For years, he was physically and emotionally gone. Right after she was murdered, we had to leave our house. Neither of us wanted to come back. Even with brand new carpet, neither of us could ever go in that room without seeing blood. Then, there were the accusations. The police didn't connect her death with the Bay River Slasher yet. That guy was long gone. They focused their investigation on my father. Husbands are always the number one suspect. Unexpectedly, family members started coming out of woodworks, telling all sorts of stories about him being abusive and them having an unhappy marriage. None of these relatives had even spoken to them in years, yet suddenly they were experts. It would have been nice if one of them took me in so I could have a somewhat normal life.

When my father was proven innocent, it changed nothing. The damage was already done. He had lost his wife, job, and family. I was all he had left, and he said he couldn't look at me without thinking back to that day. My blood-stained hands would never come clean for him. He took his life only a few months after my mother's death. I found his body floating in our new apartment's bathroom. His wrists were slashed, changing the clear water to a murky red. It was my birthday. I was just six years old, and both my parents were gone.

I was sent off to a foster home after that. I had hoped for a nice family to adopt me and I could forget about everything. It didn't happen. People knew who I was. They weren't going to take home some kid that might have issues from the murder. To be fair, they were probably right to. I had nightmares every night. I'd wake up screaming. No one was able to console me. As the years went by, I watched as other children got adopted. I was jealous, but I never felt sad to see them go. I had no friends there. They also knew who I was. Their taunts and jokes filled me with hatred. I longed to get revenge on them.

Like I longed to get revenge on the man who murdered my mother.

*****

"At eighteen, I was set up with an apartment and a shitty job. By then, I couldn't figure out how to have a normal life. I spent every waking moment thinking about finding you. I spent all my free time going over every detail in every murder. I needed to find something the police missed. Hell, I even visited several family members of victims and pretended to be a police detective. I had to find you."

"And you did. I'm right here. Now, what are you going to do?" Alex was afraid to hear the answer.

"That's the million dollar question, now isn't it?"

"Will we ever feel safe again?" the television reporter said.

"Well, Kim? Do you think you'll feel safe with me gone?" Rich's head spoke through the thin plastic of the garbage bag laying on the carpet next to her.

"Shut up."

Kim had been sitting in her living room chair for what seemed like hours. It was getting dark. She had a perfect view of the door that leads to her tenant's basement apartment. When Rich lost his job and couldn't seem to keep a steady one, they decided to rent out the basement. Rich had built a soundproof studio in the basement in case his music career ever took off, and he was sad to give it up, but it and the other storage room were perfect for bedrooms or whatever a renter wanted to use them for. There was already a bathroom downstairs, so it was just the task of putting in a small kitchen area. Right away they found someone interested when they listed it in the paper. Ben Hughes was the perfect tenant. He kept to himself and always paid his rent on time. She and Rich were happy to have him and the extra income.

Now I need him to leave.

"Last week's terrorist attack still has citizens in Spain and all over the world on edge," the reporter said. "Where will the next attack be? Will the bloodshed ever end?"

"Not if Kim has anything to say about it," Rich replied.

"Would you please shut u-"

Ben passed by the window. It didn't look like he had shaved in days, but his thin frame was unmistakable. Kim watched as he got into his car and backed out of the shared driveway. Not wasting any time, she put the hammer and nails in her jean pocket and grabbed all four trash bags by their ties. They were heavy, but she could drag them. Luckily, she did not have to go outside with Rich's body. While Ben had a door that led to the outside so he could come and go as he pleased, they still had access to the original stairway that connected the basement to the rest of the house. Normally, they kept the door off the kitchen locked with no real need to use it.

"Looks like we're returning to the scene of the crime," Rich said as his body was dragged over the kitchen tile. Blood still covered the floor and walls. After she took care of bags, she'd have to clean up in here.

"Come on, Kim. Talk to me. All good marriages are built on good communication."

Kim ignored him and unlocked the door.

"You won't get away with this, Kim. You can't just make someone disappear forever."

"Watch me," Kim said as she hurled the bags down the darkened stairwell. She took a deep breath and began to descend the steps.

Why do I suddenly have a bad feeling about this?

Chapter Eight

Minds of Maniacs

I have a bad feeling about this.

Erin knew she needed to escape and it wasn't going to be easy. She had a plan, though. The cords were tight around her wrists, but she was still able to manipulate the scabbed-over area of where her fingers used to be. She rubbed one of the wounds against her restraints until it started to bleed. It hurt, but she didn't have time to care. Erin repeated this process on all of her finger stumps and then, held them straight up. The blood slowly trickled down her palms and the back of her hands until it settled on the area of her bound wrists. Using her own blood as lubricant, she twisted and pulled, trying to free her arms. She persisted, knowing she couldn't give up. She didn't ever want to feel that man's touch again or find out what else he had planned for her. Finally, one hand slid out and then, the other.

Okay, Erin. What are you going to do about those feet?"

There were still the cords around her ankles. Without the use of her fingers, Erin wouldn't be able to get a good grip on them. She slid her body forward, giving herself plenty of slack and could finally sit up. She looked to the table in front of the bed with the silver platter of knives. It was still too far away. Then, she saw her answer.

It was between her legs.

The iron penis featured a sharp spiral of metal that led up to a point. She knew it could cut through her restraints, but she wouldn't be able to maneuver it into position from where it was. Erin reached down, placing her bloody palms on the base of the dual penis. She lifted upward, pulling on the black thread that bound it to her groin. Her hands hurt, but her crotch hurt even more as the crisscrossing stitches started to come apart, sometimes taking skin with it. The delicate flesh of that area began to bleed where Ben's needle had stabbed her before. She grunted as she pulled even harder, tugging and ripping out pubic hair.

The last thread finally broke, and the penises shot upward. Erin stopped them inches from her face. Though she knew she would miss her boyfriend, she never wanted to see his cock ever again. She pivoted the knife-like dildo over and lay its spiraled blade against one of the cords that bound her feet. Moving it back and forth in a sawing motion, the restraint finally snapped. Quickly, she maneuvered the Devil's penis over to the other rope and sawed through it.

She was free. Erin threw her feet off to the side of the bed and stood up. She instantly fell to the floor, screaming in pain. Her new cloven feet were impossible to walk with as putting pressure on them split the tear even more. She stared at them, wondering how she was going to crawl out of here when she saw her clothes under the bed. On top of them sat her shoes. Erin grabbed them and brought herself to a sitting position. She cried out as she forced her left separated foot together along the burned scabs and slid it into her shoe. She did the same to the right and then, hooked her elbow around the metal bar of the bedframe. She slowly stood up, testing her feet, before she moved away from the bed. Pain shot up her legs. Her shoes felt as if they were filling with blood, but she couldn't stop now.

She was slowly limping toward the door when she caught sight of her reflection in the silver platter. A monster stared back at her, and she couldn't take it. She didn't want to be his masterpiece anymore. She did her best to palm each finger with both hands and rip them from the skin on her cheeks and chins. She then grabbed the thumbs that were her devil horns and tore them out as well. Erin looked back in the platter and finally saw herself, though blood covered her face and chest now.

Time to get out of her.

She staggered to the door, said a little prayer, turned the knob, and slowly opened it. Peeking around the corner to the left, she saw a set of stairs going up and the bathroom where she had been when Ben made her look at herself. Looking the other way, she saw another door to a different room, what must have been his bedroom/living room, a kitchen, and what appeared to be the exit door. Before Erin could take one step past the threshold of her prison, she heard a door open.

Shit! He's back.

Erin closed the door and made her way back to the bed. Then, the silver tray caught her attention again. It wasn't her reflection that made her stop. It was the knives. She quickly grabbed the biggest one she could using both hands and went back to the door. She pressed her naked body flat against the wall and held the blade high.

I'm ready for you, asshole.

"I'm home," Gail said after she stepped through the door. The date had gone alright, but she didn't want to ruin things by sleeping with the guy too early. Maybe the next time they went out, Gail would, but until then, she liked to leave him wanting. Right now, she just wanted to get some sleep.

"Amanda?"

Gail expected the teenager to come bounding up to her, asking how her date went like she normally did. Instead, the house was silent. She left the entryway and headed into the living room, expecting to find Amanda watching television.

The first thing she noticed was the television mounted on the wall was off. The second thing she noticed was the fireplace mantle. Sitting on the shelf next to the numerous family photographs were three bloody skulls. Scraps of flesh and hair hung from the bone as gore dripped down the front brickwork of the fireplace.

It didn't dawn on Gail whose these skulls were. In a state of shock, she rounded the back of the L-shaped couch to get a closer look at the mantle. She thought that maybe it was some sort of horrible joke set up by her slightly morbid son. When her path was finally clear, she saw the severed limbs that lay all around the floor. They were positioned in multiple crude circles, their blood soaking into the white carpet. In the center, sat a large man with a meat cleaver on his lap. Long brown hair hung over his face.

Her eyes darted around at the scene before taking in everything. Some of the limbs were much smaller than the rest. It was then she knew. She tried to tell herself it wasn't true, but she knew it was. Gail collapsed onto the floor. "Harper," she whispered.

When the man stood up and walked over to her, Gail didn't even move. She had already lost the only thing that mattered to her. The man lifted her up and brushed the blond hair away from her face. Now that she was close to him, she could see his face. But it wasn't his face. She saw the same cheeks she kissed every chance

Gail got, and she saw the forehead she felt when her little boy was sick. She began to cry.

And the man hugged her.

"You. . . You look like her."

Gail didn't know what was going on. She thought for sure that he was going to kill her. Now, he was comforting her, running his hand through her hair.

"You remind me of my mom. She died a long time ago."

Suddenly, the big man was crying. Gail was repulsed as she felt him rest his head on the top of hers. Her son's dead flesh pressed against her hair. Not knowing what else to do, she hugged him back.

"It's okay. Let it all out," she said, trying to figure out her next move. The top of her head felt wet. She shuddered thinking that rather than tears, it was Harper's blood making her hair damp.

The phone in the kitchen rang. Gail longed to run over and answer it. She wanted to scream to whoever it was that she needed help. Instead, she just stood there hugging the man that killed her son, her everything. Eventually, the phone stopped ringing, and the answering machine took over.

"You've reached the Griswold residence. We're not here right now. You know what to do."

Beep.

"Hey, Gail. It's Chuck. I just wanted to tell you that I had a blast on our date and I can't wait for the next one. Talk to you later. Have a good night."

Gail felt the arms around her tense up, squeezing her body tight. "My mother didn't go on dates," the man calmly said. "My mother was happily married."

She tried to say something, anything, but his arms were crushing her, making it impossible to talk and hard to breathe.

"You are not my mother. You're just a slut that wears her face."

Gail took her head away from his chest, trying to breathe, and looked up at him, shaking her head, pleading with him that he was wrong about her.

"Give her face back."

The man's mouth lunged downward, biting down on her cheek. Screams filled the inside of Gail's head as he whipped his head side-to-side like a dog with a chew toy. Her flesh finally pulled away, and he spit the piece of flesh onto the floor. Before Gail realized what was happening, he dove in again, clamping his teeth down on her nose. The cartilage within snapped as both sides of his teeth connected. Gail managed nothing more than a wheeze as her nose sailed through the air. He continued his attack, using his teeth to rip through tendons, muscles, and skin, but Gail was already gone. Her ribs had cracked and punctured her lungs as his arms wrapped tighter around her chest and back. The last thing she saw before she died was the warped face of her son. His cheerful smile was covered in her blood.

There was something unsettling about Owen's smile. Alex didn't like the way it never wavered as he spoke. Yet at the same time, he seemed almost emotionless with his tale. For the first time in a long time, Alex felt fear.

"You made me the monster I am today. I'm a hunter. I stalk my prey and enjoy the pursuit. I'll be frank with you. Now that I have you, you're a bit of a disappointment."

"I'm a what!?"

Owen took a drink from his glass. "I wish I could have hunted you in your prime. Instead, I get this old man. I had hoped when I first found you that I was mistaken. Hell, I usually don't drink this much. I kind of need it."

Who the hell does this guy think he is?

"I may not be in my prime, but I'm still just as dangerous."

Owen roared with laughter, causing everyone in the bar to stop what they were doing for a few seconds and turn to them. "That's great. Tell you what. I'd like to see you prove that, but at the same time, no hard feelings if you can't. I'll give you a few days to decide. Fight or flight."

"What the hell are you talking about?"

"The game. The hunt. That's what I'm talking about, Mr. Bay River Slasher. Either you run, and I continue my pursuit, or we have our final showdown. The choice is yours."

"Listen here. I'm-"

"No. You listen. This is the most important decision you're ever going to make, so I'm going to give you some time to decide, but don't take too long. You'll also need some of that time to flee or prepare yourself."

"I could call the police."

"And I'd tell them about you."

Damnit.

"You know what? The Bay River Slasher is a legend," Alex said. "I don't even know who I'm facing off against. You have a famous name, Mr. Big Shot Killer?"

The cold smile never left his face. "I don't have a name. I'm sure they've connected my kills and perhaps the police have a name for me, but they have kept it quiet. Unlike you, I don't want fame. I just do it for fun. . . and in your case, revenge."

I'm no match for this guy, just like with his mom. I need to get in his head.

"Figures. All my kills are well documented. You've got nothing. You're a nobody."

Now, that smile faded. "I'll prove to you how dangerous I am. I, too, get those urges you described. While I give you time to think about your options, I'll go house-to-house killing your neighbors in the cul-de-sac you live in every night until your time is up. If I get caught or mess up, you'll go free. But I won't get caught, and unlike you, I don't make mistakes. I'll murder every last one of them and then, you'll be my dessert."

I guess I have no choice. I need more time to think.

"Fine. I'll play your game."

Owen's smile returned. "Your hand is shaking. I can see you want to run and that's fine. I found you once, and I'll find you again. You can change your name as many times as you want, David Castle. That's right. I know all about you. I have all your aliases ending with your current Alexander Richard Madison. Sometimes going by Alex. Sometimes going by Rich. Doesn't matter your name. I'll find you and take from you everything you hold dear."

Kim reached the final step and peeked around the corner. Nobody appeared to be around or noticed the bags she had tossed down the stairs. She knew no one lived with Ben, but it was possible he had visitors.

"You might not get caught today, but you will eventually."

Kim kicked the bag that held her husband's head and made her way past the bathroom and the two bedrooms. She entered the living room/kitchen area and was surprised to see a bed. She didn't understand why Ben would sleep in the living room when he had two bedrooms. Not seeing or hearing anything, she went back and grabbed the garbage bags.

"Aren't you going to even say goodbye?"

Kim ignored him, dragging Rich's body across the floor to one of the bedrooms. She grabbed the knob and twisted. It was open. Kim had a bad feeling about this, but she pushed the door open and walked inside anyway.

Shaun Hupp

Chapter Nine

Kings of Knives

The door opened as Erin watched with her body pressed against the wall. When the figure emerged from the darkness, she lunged from the wall and drove the knife downward. Ben yelped, throwing his arm up. The blade cut into his thin bicep, but Ben managed to push her away. Erin stumbled, feeling the pain in her feet. She remained standing. The knife, however, fell from her grasp. She didn't think there was any way she could get a grip on it from the floor before he got to her.

"What the hell are you doing!? What have you done?"

Erin held her fingerless hands up in front of her. If it came to it, she could slap him or try to karate chop him. "I'm getting out of here."

"All of my work. You got rid of it all. You ruined my masterpiece!"

Ben reached down and easily picked up the knife she had dropped. While he was bent over, Erin ran forward and kicked him as hard as she could in the face. Her body hit the floor as her foot exploded in blinding pain. When she regained her senses, she looked over at Ben and saw his nose was gushing blood, but he only seemed angrier. He got to his feet, looking for the knife he had grabbed, while Erin tried to stand. Putting any kind of weight on her cloven hoof made her almost pass out. She resorted to crawling on her hands and knees, trying to get to the door.

It slammed shut in front of her.

"It didn't have to end this way. I really thought you were the one."

Ben grabbed her and flipped her onto her back. Erin cried out as she saw the light reflect off the Devil's penis he held above his head. He couldn't find the knife he dropped, but Ben easily found his creation sitting on the bed. He brought the iron spike down into her throat. The spiraled edge easily punctured her neck. Her useless hands pawed at the blade as blood poured from the wound. Jake's limp cock swayed back and forth in front of her face, blood dripping with each swing. Erin shut her eyes and never opened them again.

"It's a real shame. I guess I'll have to find someone else."

"Can't you find something else to watch?"

"What?"

"Can't you put something else on the tv!?"

"What?"

Ester threw her hands up and sat back in the loveseat defeated. She hated when George didn't have his hearing aids in. For whatever reason, he had decided they weren't safe to sleep with, so he made sure to be extra careful and removed them by 8 PM every night. Ester couldn't comprehend how George spent another two hours afterward watching television religiously. She knew he couldn't hear it.

The 'it' in question was some stupid police show. It always had plenty of action and car chases. Ester supposed that you really didn't need to hear the dialogue if that's all you cared about. She also assumed that George got a kick out of the scantily clad actresses that appeared to be losing pieces of clothing with every bad guy they captured. Figuring that it had been several weeks since they fooled around and perhaps those young, curvaceous women got him going, Ester reached over and grabbed her husband's penis through his gray slacks.

It was as limp as the spaghetti she had cooked for dinner.

"What the hell is wrong with you?" George said, pushing her wrinkled hand away.

"Fine!" Ester yelled out, jumping up from the couch as fast as her elderly frame could. "You enjoy all those young tarts. I'm going to bed."

As she stormed off, she heard George say, "What?"

She, however, did not hear the massive intruder as he walked in front of her path. She screamed as the man's meat cleaver slammed down into her arms as she tried to defend herself. Ester hit the floor and tried to crawl back to George. She cried out again as the knife cut her back to ribbons with blow after blow. Only a few feet from her husband, she died in a pool of her own blood.

"What?"

George knew she was probably complaining about something, but his show was on. He grabbed the remote and turned the volume up. After having his shows interrupted for the past several days by coverage of the terrorist attack in Spain, he was glad to finally be able to enjoy his program in peace. If his wife didn't like it, she could watch tv in the bedroom.

He didn't hear as Owen stepped over his wife's lifeless body, nor did he realize that the killer silently stood right behind him. George watched the screen as one of the actresses took her shirt off to persuade a drug lord into turning himself over to the police. His eyes were glued to the tv as the cleaver sliced down the center of his bald head.

"What?" he weakly said before he fell forward onto the carpet. His brain matter oozed out of his skull.

Owen sat down on the couch and looked, not at the television, but out the window. Next door lived the man that murdered his mother. Next door was the man that ruined his life. But for now, Owen had to play the game. Alex or Rich or whatever he wanted to call himself had one more day. Either he would run, or he would fight. Owen hoped for the latter.

"I'm sorry, honey. I didn't mean to-"

"What!? You didn't mean to do what? Ruin dinner? Because that's what you did," Rich yelled as he threw the plate of food at the wall. It shattered, sending food and broken pieces of porcelain all over the floor. "Now. Clean this mess up."

Rich stormed off, leaving Kim sobbing over the sink. He went into the living room and tried to cool off. He had been snapping at his wife over the past several days, and it was getting worse and worse. Time was running out, and he still wasn't sure what to do about Owen. He really didn't want to leave town again and be on the run for the rest of his life. He had put all that behind him.

But can I fight Owen? And what about Kim?

After he had gotten home from the bar, he started packing a bag in case he needed to take off in an instant. Kim thought he had been job hunting all day. She thought that was what he had been doing most days. Instead, he was usually drinking and sometimes looking for work. While being unemployed stressed him out, it was nothing compared to having a serial killer out for your head.

I shouldn't have treated Kim like that. I still care for her, don't I?

Truth be told, Kim was basically a cover. Rich used her to hide in plain sight. Behind closed doors, she was nothing more than a punching bag for when the urges came. She took it and never went to the authorities. It was the perfect relationship for Rich. He said loved her, but he wasn't sure love was something that was even possible for him.

Rich looked back toward the kitchen. He needed to let off some steam, and he knew exactly how to do it. He clenched his fists, picturing himself punching his wife over and over. He knew it was what he needed. After he was finished with her, he would apologize and leave, saying he needed some time to himself. If Owen came to the house, he would not be there. If he killed Kim, so be it. For now, he needed to clear his head.

"Honey?" he said, walking back into the kitchen. She turned to him with tears in her eyes. Rich didn't care. "Why haven't you fucking cleaned up the floor like I told you!?"

"I. . . I-"

"I. I. I. Stop studdering, bitch! Fucking clean this shit up!"

He clenched his fists and rushed toward her. He didn't see the butcher knife until it was sticking out of his stomach. Then, the

99

pain hit him. Rich stumbled backward, the blade sliding out of his gut. Kim seemed to be in shock as much as he was. Blood poured from the wound, and Rich knew he had to call for an ambulance. He turned toward the phone and ended up slipping on something on the floor. Smacking his forehead on the tile, Rich crawled toward the wall. His head grew foggier as his hand pawed for the phone hanging on the wall. His vision started to dim as he lost more and more blood.

She finally stood up to me. It's about fucking time. Well, at least I don't have to deal with Owen.

Rich turned his head toward his wife and said, barely above a whisper, barely more than a wheeze, "Good luck."

The room was dark. Kim felt around the wall for the light switch. It had been so long since she and her husband built these additions, she couldn't remember where it was. She finally found it and flipped it.

She wished she hadn't.

Her handful of black garbage bags were nothing compared to the amount of clear trash bags that filled the room. Kim's eyes darted around the room at each. Cold, dead eyes stared back at her under the plastic. The spare bedroom was full of dead bodies in various stages of dismemberment. Air fresheners hung from the ceiling tiles like birthday streamers. Even with the fake scents and even through the thin plastic, the smell of rot and death was unmistakable.

How?

Kim couldn't believe a monster had been living in the same house as her. He had been here for less than a year and already amassed piles of bodies. It was unreal. Kim didn't want to look, but she felt the need to. She tiptoed over and sidestepped bags, looking in each. All of them were women, and a lot of the bodies had odd man-made deformities. One woman had her eyes sewn shut with black thread. Another had her teeth removed and replaced with crude, metal fangs. Kim felt dizzy as she moved among bag after bag of mutilated flesh. Another woman had a thread crisscrossing her forehead and mouth. A spiraled blade was stabbed into her neck. Kim leaned in, staring in wonder as the bag almost seemed to move. Then, she realized what it was.

Maggots.

That body and many more had been dead for quite a while. No amount of wrapping and sterilizing would keep the bugs away. Kim noticed there were fly strips on the walls. They were completely filled.

Near one of the strips, Kim saw her destination. She knew the wooden board that could be lifted away and nailed down. She didn't see much of a point anymore.

I could leave him in this room. I could put my bags underneath his bags, and I wouldn't have to worry about the smell. Hell, maybe if the police ever did find out about him, he would take the blame for Rich.

"You can't leave me in here, bitch. It's not going to get rid of me. You'll still hear me as long as you live in this house."

Weaving her way back toward the talking trash bags near the entrance, Kim went to grab them, but they had an idea. She left the bedroom, turned to her left, and went to the second bedroom.

This was the one they had built as a soundproof music studio. Kim figured if Ben was using the living room as a bedroom, perhaps this room, as unbelievable as it might be, could also be filled with dead bodies. She much rather have Rich spent the rest of his life in the soundproof room. Maybe then, she wouldn't have to listen to him. Kim opened the door. The light was already on. The room wasn't filled with dead bodies. It had one body.

And it was still alive.

"Help me."

Chapter Ten

(Un)Making the Maniacs

Owen stood in the middle of the road of the cul-de-sac, looking at all the houses that surrounded him. The sun was gone. The moon barely shined, but a sliver. Streetlamps were the only source of light. Everything was quiet. Everything and everyone was dead.

Except for one house.

Alex's car sat in the driveway. Owen was excited.

He's here. He's going to fight.

Owen stepped toward the house when he heard the rumble of a car behind him. He turned and watched as the vehicle pulled into the driveway, parking next to Alex's car. A tall, thin man got out, gave him a weird look, and then headed toward the side of the house. Owen watched as he opened a door leading to the basement. Owen was aware of the man living in the basement, but he assumed he would be gone longer than he was.

I'm not delaying any longer. Things just got more interesting.

Owen pulled out his meat cleaver and resumed walking toward his destination.

The hunt is over. Now, it is time to move in for the kill.

Kim ran over to the naked woman, leaving the bedroom (or whatever this room was) door open. She looked to be in her early twenties. Her short, black hair was drenched in sweat as was her entire body as she struggled against her binds. She was tied up like an X with her wrists and ankles bound to each corner of the bloodsoaked mattress. Her flesh was pale, but for the most part, looked unmarked. From seeing what was in the other room, Kim assumed the blood was old. She also assumed that this woman would soon be joining them.

"Help me! Get me out of here."

Seeing the table of knives at the foot of the bed, Kim grabbed one and went to the woman's right wrist. She put the blade to the cord. "Don't worry. I'll get you out of here." Just then, Kim heard the main door of the apartment open.

"Shit. I. . . I have to go."

"No! You can't leave me. Cut me out. That freak wants to turn me into a fucking art project."

"I can't. There's no time. I'll come back for you, I promise. I'll bring help."

"No. Cut me out now! I'll scream. He'll hear me. I swear I will. I'll-"

Kim saw her reflection in the knife. Her body moved again as if it was on autopilot. Dropping the blade onto the mattress, she pulled out the hammer from her pant's pocket and brought it down hard on the woman's temple. The room fell silent. A thin line of blood trickled from her forehead.

"No. . . I didn't mean to. I-"

"Kim! You've got to get out of here," her reflection in the knife's blade said. "Hurry!"

Kim ran out the door, made a lefthand turn, and flew up the stairs. Once she was in her kitchen, she spun around, closing the door behind her. Her hand went to the deadbolt and froze. She had an odd feeling that she wasn't alone in the kitchen. She slowly turned around. Standing in the center of her gore-covered kitchen was a large man. He, himself, was covered in blood. A meat cleaver hung from his right hand. Long, strands of dark, brown hair covered his face. All Kim could see was his mouth. The man smiled a smile that cut through to her very core. Then, he uttered one word: "Run."

Ben had just wanted to run out to the store for some groceries. His art took a toll on his body as he forgot to eat, sometimes for days depending on the project. He told himself that he should take better care of himself. With his fridge empty, he knew he had to go out. He tried to go out at least once a day anyway, just to get some air and clear his head. He liked going out at night too. Fewer people to interact with. Only he had forgotten to grab his wallet when he left his basement apartment. It didn't surprise him. His mind wasn't as sharp as it used to be. He feared that, like all great artists, he might be going a bit mad.

"Where the hell did I put it?"

He looked around the living room/bedroom but didn't see his wallet. A quick scan of the kitchen didn't end the search either.

Could I have dropped it in the studio?

He walked to the back of the apartment to the hallway that contained all the rooms. Ben froze as soon as he saw that both rooms were left open.

Now, I know I would never do that.

Ben went into his studio to make sure his latest canvas was still there. She was, but she wasn't moving. He rushed to her, seeing the knife on the bed and the blood and bruise on her forehead. It didn't make any sense. When he left her, she was fine. He looked around the room for any sort of answer.

"No. No. NO! What the hell is going on!?"

Someone has to be here. Someone is trying to destroy my art!

He grabbed a knife from the silver tray and ran into the other room, his gallery of failed projects. The light was on, which it usually wasn't. He almost tripped when his foot connected with a bag on the floor. There were four black bags that he knew didn't belong in there. He only used clear bags because sometimes he liked to come in here when he needed inspiration. Using the knife, he began to slice away at suspicious bags. He pulled out several mysterious, severed body parts until he found what he was looking for: the head. It was in bad shape. Most of its teeth were broken or missing. Its nose was smashed in. Still, he knew who it was.

"Why, Mr. Madison, what are you doing here? What has happened to you? You should be upstairs. Could it be a spat with the misses? Perhaps I should go check. Please, come with me."

Ben carried Rich's disembodied head by his hair, left the gallery, and headed up the rarely ever used stairwell to his landlord's house.

Kim fled the kitchen for the living room and more importantly, the front door. Her hand reached for the knob only to find that it was missing. A jagged stump of brass was all that remained. She turned back, only to see the large man barreling toward her. With no other option, she headed upstairs, taking each step two at a time. Hearing his heavy footsteps behind her, she knew she couldn't slow down, even a split second would cost her her life. She swore she felt his fingertips almost grab her hair as she rounded the corner for the hallway that led to the master bedroom. Once inside, she slammed the door and locked it. She didn't feel safe for even a moment as a monstrous blow shook the door on its hinges.

That lock will never hold. The window! I can go out the-

"No."

Kim looked around for the voice and then, finally found the source. In the mirror attached to her dresser, her reflection was waving, trying to get her attention. "You are not running anymore. You need to stop being the victim, Kim. You need to fight."

"I can't! Did you see the size of that guy? He'll kill me!"

"Let me take over again. Have I failed you yet?"

A large piece of wood hit the floor as the maniac's meat cleaver cut into the door. Kim looked back to her reflection and frantically nodded, hoping for a miracle. She had no choice. The man's huge arm broke through the upper part of the door and reached for the knob. Moving with no control of her body, Kim sprang forward with her hammer and smashed it against his hand. He screamed out but kept pawing for the lock. Kim watched as her hands flipped the tool around and she drove the claw end into the back of his hand. She drug the two sharp points down, ripping into the soft meaty tendons down to the bone. Now, his hand lashed out at her, trying to grab at Kim or her hammer. She jumped backward out of reach. Seeing, he couldn't get to her, his hand went back to searching for the door handle.

He was inches away from it when Kim returned to the door and lined up a nail to his already torn-up hand. She quickly pounded it in with the hammer. Her pursuer screamed out. Kim ignored it, striking it again and again until his hand was secured to the door. Placing another nail against the bloody tendons, she hammered in another one just in case.

Kim couldn't believe what she did next. She unlocked the door and swung it inward, bringing the man into her room being dragged by his hand. She quickly ran past him, but he stretched his foot out, tripping her. Kim hit the floor hard. The man pulled the door closed, getting within reach of her. His unharmed left hand dropped the cleaver, seized her ankle, and began to drag her back to him. Kim kicked and kicked until she got free from his grasp. She scrambled to her feet and headed toward the stairs.

I've got to get out of here!

She was within a few feet of the first step when her downstairs tenant Ben emerged from around the corner. In one hand, he held a knife. In the other, he held Rich's head that she had sawed off.

"Mrs. Madison, I believe you forgot something."

Ben held up the head. Rich winked at her and smiled. "I told you that you couldn't get rid of me that easily, Kim."

"Mrs. Madison, you know I value my privacy. That is strike one."

Kim didn't say anything. She just continued to stare at her husband's severed head. He took a step forward, and she backed away. Her eyes darted back and forth between Ben and the head.

"No. No. No. Please," she cried.

"You can't be using my gallery as a dumping ground for your garbage. That is strike two."

She looked behind her back and continued to move away from him, looking over her shoulder every so often.

"Just leave me alone!"

"But ruining my canvas? Destroying a potential masterpiece? That's unforgivable and unfortunately for you, strike three. I'm afraid I'm going to have to take matters into my own hands."

Ben heard some grunting and then, a scream of pain from down the hallway. He looked past his landlord and saw a hulking man holding his blood-covered hand. He then picked up a meat cleaver from the floor and stood. Mesmerized, Ben walked forward. Surprised, Kim jumped to the wall, pressing herself against it as he walked by her.

"And who are you?"

The large man, much like Kim, eyed the head he held. An angry grimace could be seen between the strands of hair that covered his face. "Did you kill this man?"

Ben shook his head. "No, I did not. She did. I don't kill people. I create art, Mister. . ?"

The man didn't say anything.

"Anyway, I'm an artist. Soon to be world famous. I like what I see before me. So big. So powerful. So much flesh to work with. I had it so wrong picking all those small framed women. You, sir, are the perfect canvas. I can finally create my masterpiece! What do you say?"

The meat cleaver struck Ben between the eyes, splitting his skull. His brain's synapses fired off randomly, filling his vision with a multitude of different colors.

"So. . . beautiful."

Ben fell to the floor dead and dropped Rich's head. His perfect canvas stepped over his body. Besides them, the hallway was empty. Kim was gone.

Chapter Eleven

Murdering your Maniacs

"HELP! SOMEONE HELP ME!"

Kim had gone out the side door and was now, running to her neighbor's house. She leaped onto their front porch and banged on the windows as she made her way to the door. It was locked, so she beat the door as hard as she could, trying to get their attention. Kim knew the husband was hard of hearing. She looked back toward the door she came from. After no answer, she went to the windows on the other side of the door and looked inside at the living room.

There, sitting on their couch, as they always were, was Mr. and Mrs. Saunders. Only now both of them were covered in blood, their elderly bodies slumped against one another. Kim backed away and ran to the next house.

"HELP! PLEASE!"

She tried the door and found it was locked as well. She hit the door over and over. Kim stopped to listen for any movement within. There was none. She hopped off the steps and trampled through their garden. Looking through the living room window, she gagged as she saw the ringed design of severed limbs on the floor.

This is crazy. Is everyone in the neighborhood dead?

She turned back to her house just in time to see the maniac emerge. She dropped to the ground and crawled into her neighbor's bushes. She had no idea what to do. She frantically looked around for anything reflective, trying to get advice from her doppelganger.

"Please. Tell me what to do," she whispered. "I need help. You can take over again."

No answer.

Kim watched as the man walked along the sidewalk, searching for her. She knew by the way he openly walked around covered in blood that he wasn't worried about anyone seeing him. She assumed he killed them all.

Everyone but you.

"We'll take care of that soon enough."

No. It can't be. That was Rich's voice. But where is he?

She didn't see his severed head anywhere. Last time she had saw it, her tenant was holding it before he got a meat cleaver in the head. The only thing her attacker was carrying was that same weapon. As he got closer to her, Kim gasped at what she saw under the streetlamp. Now, she knew where her husband was. The flesh of Rich's face had been torn off and attached to the large man's face.

"You can't escape me, Kim," the lips of the mask said. The mouth of the man underneath did not move.

The man continued to look for her. Kim knew she needed a plan and now, she'd have to do it without any help from the other Kim. She looked around at her neighbors' houses, trying to remember anything that might help her.

It came to her.

Kim climbed out of the bushes and sprinted toward the Campbell's residence. The maniac turned around and saw her. He chased after her, his longer legs getting him closer with each stride.

She got to the side door to their garage and flung it open. Once inside, she locked it but knew it wouldn't stop him for long. She flipped the garage's overhead light on and searched for what she needed. Brian Campbell annoyed her and the entire neighbor every weekend, but maybe his weekly task might save her life now.

It's got to be in here.

The door's frame shook hard. Kim continued her search, throwing things off shelves. She backed into a trash can, tipping it over. She stared down in horror as garbage bags hit the concrete, and two severed heads tumbled out. She recognized one as Amy Campbell, but the other had all the skin removed from its face. The blood-covered hair, however, looked like Brian's. Kim looked to her two neighbors, hoping that they would speak to her like her husband's head did, hoping they would tell her where the item she needed was.

"You can't hide, Kim!" Rich shouted as the door's frame cracked and splintered.

Finally, under a tarp, Kim found what she needed. She prayed she could get it started as the door flew open. The large man filled the doorway.

"Your time is up, Kim." The man slowly walked toward her, knowing she was trapped in the corner of the garage. "Looks like. . . Wait. No. Put that down."

Kim tugged the cord, and the chainsaw sprang to life. Its teeth spun rapidly as she swung it at the man as he reached her. The chain connected with the meat cleaver and sent it soaring across the garage.

"Kim, put that down before you hurt yourself," the mask of her husband said. The man underneath looked concerned as well. His eyes searched for some sort of weapon to defend himself.

Not letting him get the chance, Kim slashed at the maniac. Instinctively, he brought his hand up to defend himself. The chainsaw roared, ripping every finger of his right hand off. The man screamed and tried to grab her with his good hand. Kim swung the saw upwards, catching the underside of his left bicep. Another scream and the man dropped to his knees. Blood pooled out all around him.

"Get up! Don't just sit there. Kill her!" the mask desperately screamed at its wearer.

The man underneath the mask looked up at Kim defeated. "You won. The hunt is over."

Kim swung the chainsaw one last time horizontally as hard as she could, hitting him directly on the neck. The teeth sprayed blood across the walls and roared as they tried to cut through to the bone. Pulling her weapon away, the man fell forward. Unmoving, Kim released the safety bar and dropped the chainsaw.

It's over.

"It's not over. It'll never be fucking over, you bitch!" Rich yelled at her. His voice muffled slightly by the floor of the garage.

Kim screamed out this time. She lifted up the dead man's head, grabbed Rich's face, and tore it off. Then, she left her neighbor's house, heading back to her own. The skin felt warm and wet in her hand.

"What do you have in mind, Kimmy?" the piece of flesh asked as it flapped in the breeze.

114

Going back in the way she came out, Kim made her way into the kitchen. She stopped at the sink and flipped a switch. The garbage disposal turned on.

"Any last words?" Kim asked her husband.

"Go fuck yourself."

Kim pushed the piece of flesh down the garbage disposal. Rich screamed out as the blade torn apart his skin. Kim grabbed a plastic serving spoon and shoved it down the hole, making sure that every scrap of her husband was pureed.

Finally, she flipped the switch off. It was quiet. "Hello? Rich?" No response. She sighed, letting out a small chuckle.

It's finally over.

"Yes. It is."

Kim jumped back and then, tentatively took a step forward. It was her reflection in the sink. "I'm proud of you. You took both your husband and that other guy out, and you didn't even need me."

Kim smiled to herself. She was right. She did it all by herself.

"So. . ." Kim said. "Is this goodbye?"

The doppelganger nodded and then, it was nothing more than a reflection again. Kim moved her hands around in front of her face. It followed exactly what she was doing.

"Okay, Kim," she said. Now, that she had no one to talk to, she might as well start talking to herself. "Now it's time to decide what to do about all this. Should you clean up some of this mess or can you blame everything on B-"

The cold blade entered Kim's back and quickly pulled out. She grabbed the countertop to steady herself as blood flowed down her pants. Her reflection was that of pure terror and pain. She spun around only for the knife to stab into her gut.

"YOU BITCH!"

The naked woman from the basement raised the knife up and brought it down into her shoulder. "You tried to kill me and left me for that psycho!" The cords were still tied around her wrists, but a piece of rope dangled from them with frayed ends.

Kim's body slid to the floor, her blood mixing in with her husband's from earlier. The woman leaned it and stabbed her in the gut several more times. Each time, the pain lessened. Satisfied with the damage that she had done, the woman left. The room started to get darker as Kim struggled to stay awake. Her eyelids felt heavy. She laid her head against the cabinet that was under the sink. It felt so inviting like a pillow. When she finally shut her eyes, she swore she heard laughing from the pipes within.

The End?

If you want it to be, yes. If not,

turn the page for a sneak preview of. . .

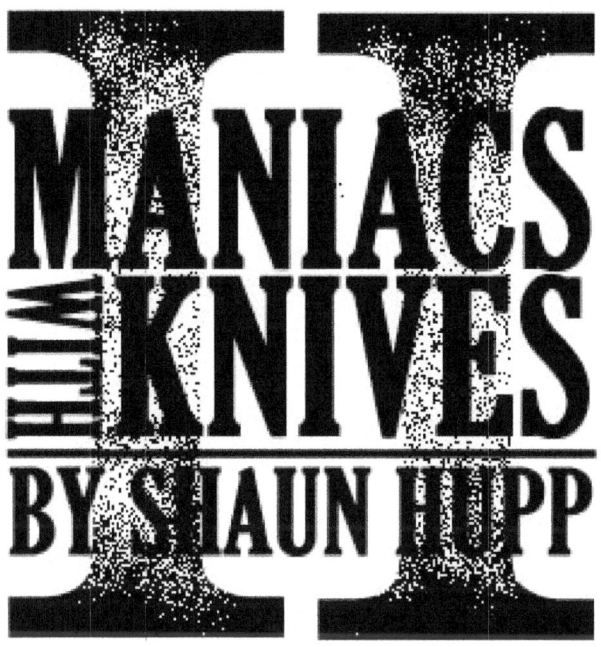

Shaun Hupp

I struggled in the dark, knowing both my arms and legs were lashed to the bedposts. Fighting a losing battle, I swore to myself that I would not give up. I thought back to all my loved ones who were counting on me. My father: He needed the extra cash I made from my fast food job to help pay the bills. My mother: She needed my emotional support as she was dealing with the recent death of her sister. My little brother: He needed me to step in as a motherly figure while ours was dealing with her own grief. I could, no, I would not let any of them down. I pulled on those thick ropes with all my might, feeling them cutting through the tender flesh of my wrists.

Before I could make any headway, a light came on, blinding me. When my eyes could finally see again, I saw the swinging bulb hanging from its chain overhead.

And then I saw her.

"Finally awake, I see. Good."

"Help me! Please! Before he comes back."

"Oh, you mean the Artist. He'll be back soon enough, and I can't wait to see what he has in store for you."

It was then that I realized that this woman wasn't there to help me. She was just as crazy as the man who kidnapped me. I pulled at the ropes in vain. I had to get out of that basement.

"There's no need for that, honey. Don't you see? You're a canvas for the Artist. He's going to turn you into a masterpiece."

The woman moved forward and placed her hand on my ankle. Slowly as she walked, she caressed my naked leg. Her hand made its way to my inner thigh. I shut my eyes as her fingers moved along my vagina before heading up my stomach. Goosebumps

121

prickled my skin as her hand moved between my breasts and ended around my throat.

"You have been chosen. This is a great honor. So, you are going to stop all this trying to escape nonsense and start showing some respect. Unless you're not worthy enough. Then, maybe my husband will deal with you."

Out of fear, I nodded. I would play along as much as I needed to. When I saw my opportunity, I would take it."

Maxine Hall shut the book in front of her and propped it up on the podium so everyone in attendance at Walter's Books could see the dust jacket. Multiple chalk outlines of bodies filled the cover. The title, "The Pleasant Ridge Street Massacre," stood out in blood red. Max's name was underneath.

"Obviously since I'm standing here today, I found that opportunity, but there's so much more inside these pages. All those psychopaths, those maniacs, their crimes and how they died are in this book; The Artist, the Bay River Slasher and his wife Kim Madison, and of course, the Skinner. I worked with the police to put together the pieces of the puzzle that were part of that crime scene."

While it was true that the police had no idea what to make of the crime scene, Maxine's assessment of the events that unfolded over that four-day stretch was merely her guesswork. Experts couldn't even figure out how everything and everyone fit. There were too many killers, too many victims, too many severed body parts, and too many murder weapons. Maxine had the only insider knowledge. However, it was seriously lacking as she had escaped after almost everyone was already dead. News reporters and the media alike tried to discredit her with facts, but Max had won over the hearts of America and the rest of the world. She was a victim and more so, a survivor. The camera ate that up, turning her fifteen minutes of fame into five years and turning her tragedy into a windfall of millions of dollars.

And for the most part, it was all bullshit. She didn't even write it. The publisher hired a ghostwriter.

"Buy my New York Times Best Selling book today and learn the history of these killers dating back twenty years ago until the day they all met for that final showdown."

The packed bookstore was on the edge of their seats. Maxine knew how to engage a room, and it was the reason she could still do book tours even after her true crime novel had been out for almost three years.

"And of course, read about how a young girl from Nebraska managed to not only escape but to be the sole survivor of that entire neighborhood. That young girl is also available for autographs. She's just not so young anymore."

She fake laughed while the audience hung on every word. She was a celebrity of happenstance. They all clapped as she descended the steps. Maxine waved them over to her table where she had a mountain of books to sell. She knew she would have no problem moving every copy.

"Mrs. Hall, I'm so excited to meet you. I've read your book about ten times."

"I can't believe I'm meeting thee Maxine Hall. My church group is going to be so jealous."

"I don't know how you did it. You were so brave. You're such an inspiration."

"Mrs. Hall, I want to be a writer just like you when I grow up."

As the line dwindled, Max looked over at her publicist. He was damn good at his job, and Max thought he was damn good in bed too. She grew tired of these local trailer trash types that flocked to her signings, but they brought in cash. She barely acknowledged the last few people asking for autographs as she stared at her lover, imagining what they would do tonight in their hotel room. As long as it didn't involve her being tied down, she would do it.

"Who should I make it out to?" Maxine asked, looking at the clock rather than the fan in front of her.

"Jamie. Jamie Camden."

Maxine froze. She knew that name. Her eyes looked up at the face of the woman that had been harassing her for years. This woman left messages on her phone, threatening her if Max didn't take back what she wrote in her book. This woman didn't just want to destroy her career. She wanted to destroy Max.

Kim Madison's sister.

"SECURI-"

The woman dropped the book, pulling a knife from within its hollowed-out pages. Before Max could call for help, the blade had entered her throat. Blood sprayed from the wound, covering the few remaining novels in front of her with a gory autograph.

"YOU KILLED MY SISTER!"

Jamie Camden climbed onto the table and pushed Maxine to the floor. She raised the knife high and brought it down again.

The fans and readers looked on as their favorite author was repeatedly stabbed in the chest, face, and neck. A generally quiet bookstore was now filled with screams.

"YOU KILLED MY SISTER! YOU KILLED MY SISTER! YOU KILLED MY SISTER!"

When Jamie was finally subdued by security, Maxine was already dead. The crowd surrounding her pulled out their camera phones, taking pictures to post online. Others used their phones to immediately jump on eBay and posted their autographed book to sell, hoping that Maxine Hall's death would be their windfall.

Thank you for reading the sneak peek of Maniacs with Knives 2. Want to read the rest? It's available on Amazon. Thank you again.

Shaun Hupp is a horror author that specializes in short stories that will tug at your heartstrings one moment and the next, shake you to your very core, sending you on an emotional rollercoaster into the darkest corners of your imagination. He loves to make his readers feel safe before jamming a rusty knife into their ribcage. Surprisingly enough, people seem to like it.

Between his wife, three children, dog, and all the characters created in his head, he's in a losing battle for his sanity and doesn't mind one bit. Growing up, Shaun was a product of watching too much Twilight Zone, Monsters, and Tales from the Darkside while reading Alvin Schwartz's Scary Stories to Tell in the Dark and R.L. Stine's Goosebumps Series over and over again, sometimes back-to-back. Later in life, he moved on to mainstream horror authors such as Richard Matheson, Stephen King, and Dean Koontz. Everything changed when he found Richard Laymon. Now, as his favorite author, Shaun asks himself whenever he writes WWRLD.

And one last time. . . Fuck you.

Printed in Great Britain
by Amazon

61004495R00078